"I knew you had a motive for coming here."

He winked. "Just not the motive you thought."

Eve responded with a roll of her eyes. He noticed her long lashes fanning the high slopes of her cheeks. In the intimate light of the inn's lobby, her caramel-colored skin was smoother than he could have ever imagined.

He wanted to make her laugh again, the way she'd laughed when they were alone in the garden. He'd wanted to take her in his arms and hold her close until she settled down.

"Incoming!"

Lost in the fantasy of holding her, he didn't quite understand what she was saying. "What's that?"

"Just...shut up."

She stepped up to him and brushed her lips to his in a whisper of a kiss. Rafael tensed, the muscles of his abdomen tightening. "Act like you're into it," she murmured.

* * *

The Rebel's Return
by Nadine Gonzalez is part of the
Texas Cattleman's Club: Fathers and Sons series.

Dear Reader,

Thank you for welcoming me to the Texas Cattleman's Club! It is an honor to join this roster of talented writers and contribute to such a celebrated series. I hope you enjoy this read and fall head over heels in love with Rafael Arias Wentworth.

For more about me, visit my website: www.nadine-gonzalez.com.

For a quick trip to Miami, Florida, without ever leaving the house, check out my latest Harlequin Desire releases: *Scandal in the VIP Suite* and *What Happens in Miami*....

To lasting love!

Nadine

NADINE GONZALEZ

THE REBEL'S RETURN

I am grateful to the editors at Harlequin Desire, Stacy Boyd and
Errin Toma, for encouraging me to join this bestselling
and beloved series, incorporating my ideas and helping me
craft these amazing characters. You are a dream team!
I look forward to a long partnership.

Thank you to my supportive agent, Jessica Alvarez. This project
helped me find you and I'm so excited for everything the future holds.

Special thanks and acknowledgment are given to
Nadine Gonzalez for her contribution to the
Texas Cattleman's Club: Fathers and Sons miniseries.

HARLEQUIN®
DESIRE™

Recycling programs
for this product may
not exist in your area.

ISBN-13: 978-1-335-73546-1

The Rebel's Return

Copyright © 2022 by Harlequin Books S.A.

For questions and comments about the quality of this book,
please contact us at CustomerService@Harlequin.com.

Harlequin Enterprises ULC
22 Adelaide St. West, 41st Floor
Toronto, Ontario M5H 4E3, Canada
www.Harlequin.com

Printed in U.S.A.

Nadine Gonzalez is a Haitian American author. A lawyer by profession, she lives in Miami, Florida, and shares her home with her Cuban American husband and their son. Nadine writes joyous contemporary romance featuring a diverse cast of characters, American, Caribbean and Latinx. She networks on Twitter, but lives on Instagram! Check out @_nadinegonzalez. For more information visit her website: nadine-gonzalez.com

Books by Nadine Gonzalez

Harlequin Desire

Miami Famous

Scandal in the VIP Suite
What Happens in Miami...

Texas Cattleman's Club: Fathers and Sons

The Rebel's Return

Harlequin Kimani Romance

Exclusively Yours
Unconditionally Mine

Visit her Author Profile page at Harlequin.com, or nadine-gonzalez.com, for more titles.

You can also find Nadine Gonzalez on Facebook, along with other Harlequin Desire authors, at Facebook.com/harlequindesireauthors.

For Ariel and Nathaniel.
You color my world.
I love you both.

A special to my sister Martine:
thanks for holding my hand through
this crazy journey.

Prologue

"It doesn't grant wishes, you know."

That pearl of wisdom was rolled out in a smooth male voice with a touch of twang. Eve Martin steeled herself against its charm. Leave it to a man to point out the blatant obvious. Yes, she was staring, mesmerized, at a multitiered champagne tower, but with good reason. Eve had started her evening staring at tap water filling a chipped porcelain mug. She'd been prepping for her nightly pity tea party when bleak hopelessness gripped her. For longer than she cared to admit, she'd watched water splash over the rim of her mug and swirl noisily down the drain, like her hopes, dreams, ambitions and every well-laid plan she'd hatched since age twelve. Once she'd been on the rise, labeled an up-and-comer in her field, 30 Under 30, and all the rest. Now she was on a Slip 'N Slide into oblivion. Well, she refused, flat out refused, to go out like that.

Stubbornness beat hopelessness any night of the week. On this Thursday night, it got her out of her pajamas and out the door and into a cab on her way to town. She'd asked the driver to take her to the only address she knew, the Texas Cattleman's Club. It wasn't until they'd pulled up to the lively venue that she understood her mistake. All she'd wanted was to enjoy a glass of wine at the bar, a simple pleasure she'd missed all those weeks in the hospital. But from the look of things, a very fancy party was underway. Eve fidgeted in the back seat, unsure of what to do next. Her driver was no help. In his late twenties, roughly her age, he wore a baseball cap and a smirk. Arms folded, he waited for her to get out of his cab. If she asked him to take her home, she would have had paid sixty dollars cash for a round trip to nowhere. God only knew she didn't have money to waste.

Ultimately, a third party settled the matter. A valet attendant stepped forward and opened the passenger door. Likely mistaking her for an invited party guest and eager to keep traffic flowing, he extended a hand. "Good evening, ma'am. Welcome to the Cattleman's Club."

With those words, she was granted access into the gilded sanctuary of Royal elite. Eve shuffled along with the others through the grand lobby to the grand ballroom. She felt lost among the chatty guests and wandered around aimlessly until she spotted the colossal champagne tower at the center of the room. She drifted toward it and watched, mesmerized, as an attendant atop a ladder poured bottle after bottle over a pyramid of long-stemmed glasses. From tap water to sparkling champagne, her night was looking up. Who knew? She might even have some fun tonight.

"It doesn't grant wishes, you know."

One glance at the wise guy was all it took to disprove that statement. Standing beside her in a well-cut navy suit, hands in pockets, head tilted to better catch her eye, was a tall man with dark hair, buttery brown skin, and brown eyes that outsparkled the best sparkling wines. For someone, somewhere, he was most definitely a wish come true.

From atop the ladder, the attendant raised the last bottle of champagne with a flourish. "Cheers, everyone!"

Eve did not need any more prompting than that. Suddenly very thirsty, she reached for a glass. To her horror, the entire champagne edifice came crashing down. Shattered glass turned the air around her into a glistening prism. Champagne splashed onto her cherry-red dress. Champagne dowsed her shoes, swirled around her ankles and flowed between her legs. Shocked, her own glass slipped from her hand and shattered at her feet.

While everyone around her scattered, she stood rooted in place. When would she learn? Stubbornness trumped hopelessness, but nothing was stronger than fate. Eve should have known better than to leave the safety of her bunker and tempt fate tonight. Her only wish now was to disappear.

One

Love at first sight was for suckers, right? In any event, that was the hill that Rafael Arias Wentworth was prepared to die on until he'd laid eyes on her. She stood motionless, staring at a champagne tower at the center of the grand ballroom. She was striking in a candy-red dress and hair gathered low in a cinnamon bun, yet all he saw was smooth, rich caramel skin. Who among this who's who of Royal was she?

Rafael reasoned away the feelings she inspired. He was still flying high from another experience. Earlier this evening, he had driven to the outskirts of town to visit a car dealer. Not the type who sold family-friendly sedans in an air-conditioned showroom. This one invited private customers into a nondescript building surrounded by a chain-link fence and guarded by massive dogs that turned out to be sweethearts. The owner was a young guy named Manny Suarez, a high-end car restorer. Rafael had reached out to him from Miami weeks before he'd decided to come back to town. Now it seemed they'd found the perfect car. After patiently answering about fifty questions, Manny told Rafael to put up or shut up. Rafael did not hesitate. He dropped a quarter of a million dollars on a 1969 Camaro convertible. He would have kicked the tires, but there were none. The rusted tin can rested on cinder blocks. It looked as if it had been drawn out of a lake. Its beauty, however, was untarnished.

He'd left the dealer's garage feeling energized. Running late for the cocktail party at the TCC, he gunned through the streets of Royal. He drove an expertly restored 1972 Jaguar XK-E. Classic convertibles were his weakness. Apparently, so were women in red.

Tonight's party was a business obligation. Rafael could not skip it, but he had no intention of staying late. He had a plan for these sorts of events: grab a drink, make the rounds and then slip out, hopefully unnoticed. But then he saw her and...*bam!*

Love or not, he was going to pass. There was only so much room in a man's heart, and tonight he'd fallen for the classic lines of a vintage Chevrolet. He dropped his glass of tequila and lime on the tray of a passing attendant. He was leaving before he did anything stupid, but not before getting the name of his sweet, caramel candy apple. That would be useful information in case he were up for falling in love some other night.

He approached her, ready to say hello. She didn't notice. She stood staring at the champagne pouring down the pyramid. He said the first thing that came to mind. "It doesn't grant wishes, you know." All he'd wanted was to coax a smile out of her. Instead, she'd glared at him. Then two things happened in quick succession, like thunder following lightning. A ladder crashed into the tower. The tower collapsed. The crash. The crunch of glass. The splash of champagne. Rafael was oblivious to it all. He recognized this woman. She was without a doubt the infamous Evelyn Martin. A part of him must have known. The feeling she'd stirred in him wasn't love, but something just as violent.

There was no time to dwell on any of it. All hell broke loose in the ballroom. Beside him, a man dabbed frantically at his suit with a cocktail napkin. A woman bemoaned the state of her designer shoes. But Eve Martin stood unflinching in the face of catastrophe, and Rafael had to admit there was something badass about that. Even so, she couldn't stay here.

"Come with me." He draped an arm around her rigid shoulders and dragged her along. He marched her out of the ballroom, her eyes downcast, her jaw and neck tight with tension. In the lobby, he asked if she was okay. No answer. Was she in shock?

"Talk to me," he said. "Say something so I know you're alright."

She took a deep breath, as if bracing to face a firing squad. "I'm going to die of embarrassment."

"Is that all?" he said. "I'll call off the paramedics then."

She dabbed her wet forehead with her fingers. "I'm a wreck."

He had a feeling this statement had more to do with her state of mind than her appearance. "Would you like to go to the ladies' room to clean up?"

She shook her head. "No."

Staff members had cordoned off the grand hall. Others were handing out towels to the soaked guests. He grabbed two and handed her one.

"It was an accident," she said, her voice catching.

He wiped his hands dry. "A freak accident."

She bunched the towel to her chest. "I didn't mean to…"

Rafael narrowed his eyes. "Didn't mean to…what?" He laughed. "You think you're to blame?"

"I grabbed a glass!"

"That's how it works," he said. "They pour the wine, you grab a glass."

"I might've grabbed it the wrong way."

She had either a martyr complex or just a warped sense of reality. "Sorry to break it to you, Calamity Jane. You're not that powerful."

"What happened then?"

"The ladder toppled over."

"Oh…"

"Oh, yeah," he said. "It was dramatic as hell. Sorry you missed it."

"That's okay," she said with a sigh of relief. "I've had enough drama. Thanks."

"I think we're done here." Rafael slipped his phone out of his pocket, ready to text his code to the valet. "What's your valet code? I'll have them bring your car around."

"Never mind. I'll grab a cab."

He pocketed his phone. "Do you need a ride? I'll take you home."

"No," she said firmly. "I'm fine. Thanks."

"You're not fine," he said. "You're soaking wet."

"My feet are wet. I think I'll survive."

"Don't be so sure," Rafael said. "If my darling grandmother is right, you'll catch pneumonia and die in twenty-four hours."

"Your darling grandmother is wrong. And you've done enough tonight. Thanks."

"Before you go handing me a medal, Evelyn, you should know that I'm using you as a shield."

The sparkle in her eyes fizzled out. "You know who I am?"

Rafael didn't answer. She really shouldn't be surprised. Everyone in town had read up on her. They knew exactly who she was and were likely keeping tabs on her, down to her address and Social Security number. Having people know you, or think they did, by reputation or otherwise, was not a good feeling. He knew it well.

"And who are you?" she asked.

There was no time to answer. Paul and Jennifer Carlton, of Carlton Realty Group, P&J for short, were fast approaching. "I'm going to whisper something in your ear. Do you mind?"

She opened wide eyes. "I'm confused. Why, exactly?"

"I need your help." He lowered his head and whispered in such a way that an onlooker might suppose they were engaged in a private conversation and back off. "Pretend we're deep in conversation. Act like you're into it."

"I'll do my best," she said.

His plan failed. The elegant couple that he was trying to avoid accosted him with air kisses, shoulder clasps and prying questions. "Rafael!" they cried in unison.

Evelyn swiveled around. "Rafael…" Recognition dawned.

"Is it true you're sniffing at the Richardson property?" Paul asked.

Rafael skirted the question. "Paul, Jennifer, have you met Evelyn Martin?"

A cursory acknowledgment before resuming their interrogation.

"Many of our clients are interested in that property," Jennifer said. "If the motel goes on the market, get ready for a bidding war."

Paul had a suggestion. "How about we grab a drink and discuss this inside."

Evelyn spoke up in a clear voice. "Sorry, we're leaving. There's been a freak accident."

The *"we"* undid him.

"Oh?" Jennifer eyed Evelyn as if she'd just teleported in and hadn't been standing there the whole time. "What happened? And why is your dress all wet?"

"A champagne tower collapsed," Eve replied.

"Goodness!" Jennifer exclaimed.

Rafael spotted the tiny beads of liquid that added shimmer to Evelyn's otherwise unadorned sheath. "We need to get you out of that dress."

She shot him a look. Okay, he conceded. This time the "we" was overkill.

"Just take me home, please," she said to him. "I can manage the rest on my own."

Paul's and Jennifer's heads turned with each response that he and Evelyn volleyed at each other. Rafael had to get rid of them. That pair traded in gossip. Pretty soon all of Royal would be making up stories. He'd been down that road before.

"I should take Evelyn home before she catches pneumonia," he said. "Nice seeing you two."

"Good night," they said.

Rafael watched them go. "Ready?"

Evelyn looked as if she were still weighing her options. He caught the exact moment she gave in. "Sure," she said. "Tonight is a bust. Lead the way."

Her words were soaked in disappointment. Rafael felt for her. She hadn't gone through the trouble of coming out just for her night to end like this. That wasn't right. He looked around and spotted a server wandering about with a tray of champagne glasses. He waved him over, grabbed a flute and offered it to her. "You deserve it."

She hesitated before taking the glass. "I thought we were leaving."

"In a moment," he said. "The valet will send word when my car is ready. In the meantime, I know just the spot where we can wait. Follow me."

Two

Rafael Wentworth was crisp like money. Was it any wonder? He belonged to one of the oldest families in Royal, going back generations. Eve wasn't an expert in all things Royal—that was her sister Arielle's wheelhouse—but that much she knew. Cammie Wentworth had very generously taken in Eve's nephew while she was indisposed. Rafael's name had clout, and he knew it. He hadn't bothered to introduce himself because he'd assumed she knew who he was.

Rafael had asked her to follow him and she had, no questions asked. He led her out a side door and down a trail to a far-off bench under a magnolia tree. Moments later, Eve found herself sipping champagne under the wide Texas sky in the company of an heir to a great fortune. It was the last day of a very long, very taxing January. The night was balmy. He slipped off his jacket and draped it over her shoulders. "I like how you handled P&J."

"You mean that couple? Is that what you call them?"

"It's what everybody calls them."

She frowned. "Somehow, I doubt it. They seemed harmless enough."

"You naive little thing."

"I'm anything but that."

"Okay, then," he said. "Can't deny we make a good team. Maybe it's our South Florida connection."

"Do we have a South Florida connection?"

"So everyone keeps telling me."

Admittedly, she knew very little about the man except that for a while he was a person of interest in the delicate matter that had brought her to Texas in the first place. He had quickly cleared his name, but Eve should have known that wouldn't be the last she'd hear of him. After all, he was Cammie Wentworth's brother. Cammie was one of the first people Eve had met in town, and their lives remained entangled to this day.

"Don't read too much into it," Eve said, trying not to read too much into it herself. "Miami has a way of making bedfellows out of total strangers."

He cracked a smile. "I couldn't have said it better myself."

Eve pulled her phone from her purse, tapped on the navigation app and handed it to him. "Take me to this address and we'll call it even."

He only glanced at the screen. "I just left that area."

What was a Wentworth doing way out in her neck of the woods? "Really? What were you up to?"

His smile grew sly. "One day, if you're good, I'll tell you."

Eve smiled, too, for the first time in…what? Six months? It made her cheeks ache. "May I ask you something?"

"Shoot."

"Why did you come out tonight? You obviously don't want to be here."

He let out a heavy sigh. "It's the cost of doing business in this town."

Eve raised her champagne glass. Moonlight danced in the bubbles. "Is it really such a burden?"

"I think so," he replied. "At the end of a long day, the last thing I want is to stand around making small talk."

He sat with his elbows on his knees and his hands folded under his chin. She couldn't help but think of those Renaissance statues, perfectly symmetrical, exquisitely chiseled. "So, what *do* you want?"

"A steak, a bottle of red, a cigar…my bed."

It all sounded so good. What she would give for all those things, minus the cigar.

"I'm curious," he said. "What did *you* come out for?"

"I wanted to have fun."

What else could she say? After months in a hospital, she had wanted to wear her old clothes and feel like her old vibrant self. That would be giving too much away. Most people didn't need a profound reason to head out for a drink on a beautiful night.

"Fun?" he said, leaning into the word as if he had difficulty catching its meaning.

She spelled it out for him. *"F-U-N."*

"I'll let you in on this secret." His voice dipped to a smoky whisper. "No one has ever had fun at a country club. It's not allowed."

"That's not true! It's beautiful here."

Music and chatter wafted their way. The party had

resumed. No one would allow a puddle of champagne to wash out the night.

Rafael got up and pulled on the knot of his tie. "That's how they get you. But don't be fooled. This club is for small talk and social climbing. That's all."

"You're crazy."

"Darling, it's Texas law," he said with a tip of an imaginary Stetson hat.

Eve let out a thin peal of laughter, and that in and of itself was a minor miracle. This morning she had cried in her coffee. These last few months had been so trying. She'd lost her sense of humor, her ability to laugh at herself and others.

"Think I'm kidding? Check the TCC bylaws," he said. "It specifically states no member shall have any fun of any kind. They'll escort you out if you do."

"I'm not a member, so I'm in the clear."

"You're not?" he said, rolling up his sleeves. With the moonlight streaming on him, adding a streak of silver to his ink-black hair, he was, possibly, the most beautiful man that she had ever set eyes on. "How did you get in?"

She'd just…walked in. It didn't occur to her that the club wasn't open to the general public. Eve took her glass to her lips and tried to hide her panic. Would they escort her off the premises now?

At first, Rafael didn't seem particularly invested in her answer. When her silence dragged on, though, his interest grew. "Evelyn," he said, "is there something you're not telling me?"

"I go by Eve, not Evelyn."

Eve was suddenly very hot. It didn't help that her damp dress clung to her body like plastic wrap.

"Eve," he said. "What are you not telling me?"

"I didn't know the rules," she said in her defense. "The only club I belong to is a gym."

"So...what did you do to get in?"

"I didn't do anything!" she said heatedly. "My cab pulled up around front. It was holding up traffic and the doorman whisked me in."

"He *whisked* you." He laughed, the smooth, rich laughter that was stored in oak barrels for decades, only to be shared with the best of friends. It left Eve feeling a little drunk. "This is so good I need popcorn."

"Oh, stop!" Eve punctuated her cry with a stomp of the foot. The soggy sole of her stilettos made an unpleasant swish sound. She slipped them off and wiggled her toes in the grass. Might as well get comfortable, too.

"Eve Martin, you are a wild woman."

She wasn't. That was the thing. She was the definition of boring and stable and predictable. Her little sister, Arielle, was the fun and spontaneous one. At the thought of Arielle, a ball of pain hardened in Eve's chest. She took a long sip of champagne to ease it down.

"Actually," he said, "I kind of like you."

Well, that was kind of nice. "I like you, too."

"You know what?" he said. "I wonder if we could marry our two visions for tonight."

True to her nature, Eve stomped a spark of interest just as quickly as it flared. "We can't marry anything."

"That's a shame," he said. "I just had a great idea."

So many warning bells were chiming, she could hardly hear her own thoughts. "What is it?"

He looked into the distance and pointed west. "I'd like to take you there."

She strained her neck and spotted a grand house on a

hill. Light poured out from every window. It looked inviting enough, the sort of place that might serve a hearty farm-to-table dinner. Was that the plan? A late meal?

"I'm not going anywhere with you," Eve said. "I'm a mess."

She yearned for her bed. Which bed, though? Not the lumpy one at the Airbnb or the hard one she'd left behind in Miami. Certainly not the hospital bed she'd been confined to for weeks upon arriving in Royal. There it was. She was bone tired and didn't have a comfortable place to rest. That was the root of her problem.

"You're not a mess, and even if you were it wouldn't be a problem," he said. "It's an inn."

Eve fell straight through the trapdoor of her imagination. What was he thinking? "If you think this night ends with us in a hotel room, you're out of your mind."

"It's not a hotel," he said. "It's an inn. Trust me, I know the difference."

It was a room with a bed. "Are you trying to say people don't have sex in *inns*?"

"They do," he said, unfazed. "But only in the dark and in the missionary position."

"What?" A dam cracked, and laughter cascaded freely from her. It felt so good to laugh again, almost like flying. "What rule book are you reading from?"

He joined her on the bench. "Do you trust me, Eve?"

"No," she said. "I don't."

Eve didn't trust him, but she wanted to trace the line of his jaw with her fingertips. One thing had nothing to do with the other.

"Could you try? For one night."

"No." Her mother, and her grandmother, for that matter, didn't raise a fool.

"That's fair," he said. "But do you know what's waiting for us over at the Belleview Inn?" he said. "A steam shower, room service, laundry service, TV, Wi-Fi and a balcony with a view of a rose garden. We can have dinner and engage in adult conversation. Does any of that appeal to you?"

All of it appealed to her. Following her hospital stay, Eve was referred to rehabilitative therapy. She was only three weeks into an arduous course of physical therapy and had pushed her body beyond its limits tonight. She felt drained, exhausted. And she was wet and hungry. She needed a shower. Room service, even at a modest inn, sounded decadent. Although she knew better than to say yes when a charming man invited her up to a hotel, motel, or a Holiday Inn, that was exactly what she intended to do. She blamed the champagne, the preferred elixir of the god of bad choices.

Rafael checked his phone. "My car is ready. What do you say?"

"I say let's go."

"Fearless," he said, almost to himself. "I like it."

They walked to the valet station where the car was waiting. Rafael Wentworth drove a classic sports car, the type only seen in films set in Italy. It suited him perfectly. He held open the door for her, then got behind the wheel. "You've had enough excitement," he said, revving up the engine. "Let's get you out of here."

They drove off into the night, leaving the Texas Cattleman's Club behind.

Three

After arriving at the inn, Eve fidgeted in the passenger seat. Rafael wondered if she were having second thoughts. He was a hotelier by profession and could not drive by a property without checking it out. They needed a shower and a good meal. A room at the nearby inn was a practical solution. If she didn't feel comfortable, he was prepared to drive her home.

"Hey," he said. "We can leave."

She froze, her hand on the door handle. "But…we just got here."

"You look uncomfortable."

"I need to get out of this dress, that's all."

"And a little nervous, too."

She waved away his concerns. "It's just how I look."

That wasn't true. He'd seen her scared, shocked and amused. Never, in the arguably short time he'd known her, had he seen her look this antsy, and he didn't like it. "You really can trust me, Eve," he said. "I've been accused of getting one Martin sister pregnant. I'm not trying to push my luck."

Her hand fell away from the door handle and she looked all at once scared, shocked and not in the least amused.

Rafael rushed to apologize, only managing to spit out a limp string of words. "Oh, shit, sorry. I didn't mean that."

But as his wise maternal grandmother would have said, *Lo que sale de la boca, del corazón sale.* Things that come out of the mouth come from the heart. He'd thought he was over the whole Royal mystery baby mess. Apparently, he was still pissed and resentful as hell. His resentment extended to the whole blessed town.

Rafael hadn't been back in Royal since leaving for Florida in a huff at age seventeen. He'd returned at the request of his family. His father, Tobias Wentworth, who was the reason he'd left home in the first place, was turning a leaf and wanted to reconcile. Although he wanted nothing more than to leave the past behind him, he'd finally relented. Naturally, Royal welcomed him with a scandal.

Not long ago, his half sister, Cammie, and her fiancé, Drake, had taken custody of an abandoned baby. All that was well and good and had nothing to do with him. While Drake and Cammie fostered the child, authorities worked to track down the baby's parents. Normally, he would have applauded the effort except, for some reason, his name topped their list.

The child was the son of Arielle Martin, a budding

freelance photojournalist from South Florida who had reached out to him a few times seeking a comment on a story. As small-town logic would have it, that connection was enough to make him the father of her infant son. Rafael hadn't wasted any time and cleared his name with a paternity test. It was water under the bridge now—except he was about to book a room with Arielle's sister, the very woman who had brought the baby to Royal in search of his father.

This could very well be a bad idea.

Eve released her seat belt with a snap. "We're going inside. I want the night you promised. Do you understand?"

It was an order. Normally, Rafael did not respond well to orders. This time, he did not hesitate. "Yes, ma'am."

At the front desk, the night manager recognized Rafael and made a fuss, offering a free upgrade to a suite.

"A two-bedroom suite," Eve insisted.

The manager reassured her. "Two very separate rooms, ma'am. Please wait here a moment. I'll be right back."

He went off to program their key cards. Eve eyed Rafael with suspicion. "Why was he fawning over you? Are you a frequent flyer or something?"

"A professional courtesy," Rafael replied. "I'm in the hospitality business."

"Interesting," she said. "I didn't know."

"I'm opening a luxury guest ranch in town with accommodations similar to this, but better."

"You're here to check out the competition, aren't you?"

He raised a finger to his lips. "Shh."

She smiled. "Sneaky… I knew you had a motive for coming here."

He winked. "Just not the motive you thought."

She rolled her eyes. Her long lashes fanned the high slopes of her cheeks. In the intimate light of the inn's lobby, her caramel-colored skin was smoother than Rafael could have ever imagined. She was of average height, reaching his chin and no higher, and she was thin to the point of frail. A good gust of wind could knock her over. Then he recalled that she was in the hospital those weeks that he was being ruled out as her nephew's father. She must have had a rough time.

Rafael was glad the tension that had built up in the car was subsiding. He wanted to make her laugh again, the way she'd laughed when they were alone in the garden. Her laughter had leaped out as if springing from a sealed cave. He'd wanted to take her in his arms and hold her close until she settled down.

"Incoming!"

Lost in the fantasy of holding her, he didn't quite understand what she was saying. "What's that?"

"Just…shut up."

She stepped up to him and brushed her lips to his in a whisper of a kiss. Rafael tensed, the muscles of his abdomen tightening. "Act like you're into it," she murmured through clenched teeth. With every nerve ending in his body setting off sparks, he didn't have to rely on dormant acting skills. He pulled her close and kissed her hard, deep, and slow. She gripped the lapel of his suit jacket and opened to his kiss. He heard her groan just before she tore herself away.

"I think we're good," she said, her voice shaky.

He was shaken, too. "How the hell do you figure?"

"I kissed you to create a distraction," she said. "P&J just walked in."

Paul and Jennifer Carlton were the most annoying couple in Texas, but at this moment he was making plans to send them a fruit basket and a bottle of wine.

"Here I thought you wanted to test that sex-in-an-inn theory."

"Stop thinking that," she scolded. "They're right over there. Don't look now, though."

He wouldn't dream of it. Her swollen lips had his undivided attention.

"Okay… They've entered the dining hall. You can look now."

"Nah. I'll take your word for it."

The manager returned. He was a little red in the face from what he'd undoubtedly witnessed.

Rafael plucked the key cards from his hand. "I'll take those. Thanks."

"Anything else, sir?"

"Send up laundry services, will you?" Rafael said. "And your best bottle of tequila."

The manager cleared his throat. "Certainly, sir. Enjoy your evening."

Four

In the elevator, Eve kept her eyes pinned to the tip of her pointed-toe stilettos. She could lie to him, not herself. The truth thrashed around in her chest. She had wanted to kiss him. All night, she had wanted to kiss that smart mouth, mess his hair and breathe in the scent of his skin. She'd seized on the flimsiest excuse to do it. It was as simple as that.

Now she stood as far away from him as physically possible. They rode to the top floor in unyielding silence. Just as the doors were about to split open, Rafael slammed on a button and the doors jammed in place. She startled and looked up at him.

"Listen, I…" His voice trailed off. She darted a glance his way. He looked as uncomfortable as she felt. "That was a really shitty thing for me to say about your sister, and I'm sorry."

"Alright."

Eve hoped he wasn't waiting for a more nuanced response. His quip about Arielle had stung. For a moment she'd panicked, not knowing what to do or say. Apart from the police and journalists still on the case, no one openly discussed Arielle. She was the stranger, the outsider, who had blown into town to dig up old secrets and stir up past resentments before mysteriously taking off.

"I never met your sister," he said. "She'd reached out to me, twice, requesting an interview. Each time I turned her down. She wanted to dig into my past, my ties to Royal and the Wentworth family. I don't want to think about my past, let alone meet with a stranger and discuss it over coffee."

Her sister was a photojournalist with dreams of someday having features in *Vogue* and *Time*. She had come to Royal to investigate a 110-year-old story with ties to the country club that was the beating heart of the town. To support herself while in Royal, her sister had taken a job at an assisted living facility. According to her diary, she became interested in one of the residents with a storied past. "I think she was more interested in Harmon Wentworth than you... Is he your great-uncle?"

"We're related, but we're not close."

"She was all about small-town America. I guess she was trying to find out what made Royal so special—and probably dig up any secrets or scandals along the way."

Rafael's lips curled with a sardonic smile. "There are enough family rifts in Royal to fill an encyclopedia."

"So I gather."

"Anyway, I am sorry." He lifted his thumb off the button. Eve rushed to press it, freezing the elevator in place. He searched her face. "What's going on?"

"I just want to say, it's alright. Apology accepted." Eve felt sorry for everyone who had been dragged into her sister's drama. Somehow, Arielle's personal choices had become everyone's problem to solve, including Eve. It was maddening and frustrating and yet, as one of her sister's two surviving relatives, Eve had no choice in the matter. There was no way out for her; she was duty bound to see this through to the end.

"But are *we* alright?" he asked.

"We're fine." She released the button. "Now let's get off this elevator."

She followed him down a quiet hall to their suite. He unlocked the door, switched on the lights and dropped the key card on the console table in the foyer. She rushed in ahead of him. "I love it."

"It's not bad," he said.

The layout was simple. The two bedrooms opened to a common sitting area. The decor was traditional and tasteful. Bay windows offered views of a sprawling garden.

"We should take notes." Eve went to the writing desk and picked up a pad and pen. "First impression—views are to die for," she murmured as she wrote.

"You're being generous."

She capped the pen. "You're being a hard-ass."

"It's just rolling grass." Rafael flung open the door of the hall closet, found a terry-cloth robe and handed it to her. It was soft. She couldn't wait to slip it on. "Need help with that dress?"

"Actually, yes." She turned on her heel and gave him her back. "Help me with the zipper."

She could use an extra set of hands. It had been such a pain to pull up.

When he gripped the tab, her breath caught. He took his damn sweet time inching the zipper down and sending a thrill up her spine. Not trusting her voice, Eve thanked him with a curt nod. Then, clutching the robe to her chest, she scurried off and locked herself in one of the bedrooms.

In the en suite bathroom, Eve gingerly stepped out of the stiff red dress and let it collapse onto the marble tile floor. She let down her hair, also stiff with styling products. She was working on releasing her bra when she heard the knock on the bedroom door.

"Yes?" She peered at Rafael through a narrow crack of the door. She had grabbed a towel and wrapped it around her torso, but with the memory of their kiss still expanding in her mind, she might as well be naked.

Rafael's gaze swept down her throat and across her bare shoulders. "Hand over the dress. Laundry service is here."

Eve slammed the door in his face. She rushed to the bathroom, picked the dress off the floor and carefully rolled it into a ball. At this point, it was a biohazard and ought to be bagged and labeled as such. Rafael was leaning casually against the doorframe when she returned. She handed him the dress through the crack. "Here you go."

"Thank you, miss," he said. "I'm ordering dinner. How do you take your steak?"

Oh, God… Just the thought of a good steak made her mouth water. "Actually…I'll have a grilled salmon and asparagus."

"Really?"

"Yup."

"Is that what you want?"

"No. It's what I should have."

"Any reason?"

"Just…trying to clean up my diet."

There was no way to bring up her new heart-healthy diet without dampening the mood.

"You're disciplined," he said. "There are plenty things I'd like to try, but I'm not starting tonight."

Maybe a little too disciplined, she thought with a frown.

"Are you sure?" he said. "It's okay to change your mind."

"Fine! I want the steak," she blurted. "Medium well."

"Medium rare," he said with a grin. "You can trust me on this. I know beef."

Trust was the theme of the night, she thought, as she slammed the door in his face for the second time.

Five

The shower was strong. Hot water needled Eve's shoulders and back, but did nothing to ease the tension in her muscles. She tried wiping the slate clean of all thoughts of Rafael: his face, his inky-black hair, warm almond skin, his fingers around her wrist, or working the zipper down her spine. And then there was that kiss. Eve pressed her forehead to the glass shower door and relived the moment the fake kiss had turned real.

She was in a hotel, no, an inn, with a gorgeous man who touched her, who kissed her, in such a way it made her melt. What was she doing hiding behind locked doors? Eve stepped out of the shower and toweled off. If she could change her mind about the steak, couldn't she change her mind about other things?

Rafael wasn't in the sitting room when she stepped out in her robe. Eve heard the shower running in the adjoining bedroom. She picked up the pad off the coffee table, curled up on the couch and added to her list.

Robe: super soft.

Complimentary toiletries: top notch!

A moment later, the door to his bedroom swung open and Rafael came out, barefoot and wearing a robe that was larger than hers. Stripped down like this, he looked more relaxed than he had all night. More touchable, too.

"You look cozy," he said.

Eve tucked her feet beneath her. "People may not come here for wild sex, but the robes make up for it."

"Ha!" he said. "You should add that to your list."

She held up the pad. "It's all here."

"May I see?" She handed it to him and he silently reviewed the growing list. "You have an interesting rating scale."

"I'm not in the hospitality industry," Eve said. "My first impression is that of the average guest."

"Very useful."

"What properties do you own?"

He dropped the pad on the coffee table. "Miami Sky and Sky Blu in Fort Lauderdale."

"Are you kidding?" Those were two trendy and frankly sexy South Florida landmarks. Miami Sky was the preferred spot for after work drinks with colleagues. Not that she'd be hanging out with colleagues anytime soon. "Why haven't I ever heard of you before coming to Royal?"

"I'm not the attraction."

She wasn't sure about that. Looking up at him now, all she saw was damp, smooth, golden skin. He was hard to miss. Although he claimed to have never met Arielle, Eve wondered if her sister had ever crossed paths with him. She must have attended those famous Sky Blu pool parties.

There was a knock and a voice announced room service. Rafael raised his eyebrows, his excitement palpable. "Are you ready to eat?"

She was more than ready. "Can't wait."

The food at the Belleview Inn was phenomenal. Either the chef was a genius or Eve hadn't had a decent meal in far too long. After dinner, she updated her list. *Food: fabulous!*

Rafael shook his head. "You're too easily impressed."

"Says the man who wolfed down his steak!"

They migrated to the couch to savor slices of tres leches cake. Rafael had insisted on dessert. Later, he asked, "Have I done right by you?"

She dragged a finger through the icing and took it to her lips. "I think so."

He set down his plate and stretched out, all long limbs and languid gestures. "Now it's time for some adult conversation."

Eve fidgeted with the knot of her robe. "I think I'll pass on that."

"Sorry. That's not an option," he said. "Review the minutes. It's on tonight's agenda."

That agenda was trash. "I've got an idea. How about we write a new one?"

"No chance," he said. "I have questions that I want answered."

"Was that your plan all along? Feed me and get me to talk?"

"It's a good plan. Works every time."

And it looked like it was going to work now. "What do you want to know?"

"Who are you, Eve Martin? Aside from the mystery woman who showed up in Royal with the mystery baby?"

According to her medical chart, she was a Black, unmarried, college-educated female, age 28, with a family history of coronary artery disease and a recently diagnosed heart defect that had landed her in a coma. None of that was sexy, thrilling, or exciting—all things she wanted to be tonight.

"Go on," he said.

She bought herself some time. "You first."

"Me? Depends on who you ask."

"I'm asking you," she said. "Maybe I was too quick to size you up. Seems to me you're a good guy."

Rafael used a cloth napkin to dab at cake crumbs on her chin. It reminded Eve of the way he'd tended to her in the club lobby, so unexpectedly tender. "I'm not all that good," he said softly.

"You've been good to me."

All her adult life, Eve had avoided men like Rafael. She'd played it smart and chosen her dates from a pool of "nice guys." What she'd gotten was a string of dull dates and lukewarm sex—no crazy night escapades or kisses that made her head spin.

He got up from the couch and returned with the bottle of tequila and the bowl of lime wedges that room service had delivered earlier. He filled two tumbler glasses with ice and set up a bar on the coffee table. "I brought you here, kept you up past your bedtime, made you eat steak, drink—" he poured her a glass "—and drink some more."

She took the glass from him, their fingers brushing.

The ice and the tequila sparkled in the overhead light. "You forget I made some decisions along the way."

"I'm just saying." He sank down to the carpeted floor and reclined against an armchair. "Maybe don't let your guard down around me."

Eve slid off the couch and joined him on the floor. "I'll make my own mistakes, thank you very much."

He raised his glass. *"Salud!"*

"Cheers." She took a sip of tequila. The chilled spirit warmed her heart.

"Were you and your sister close?" Rafael asked.

"We were sisters," she said with a sigh. "Nothing could change that, obviously. But we weren't exactly close."

"It's the same with my half sister," he said. "But we're trying."

Eve joined her hands on her lap. Since he'd brought up Cammie, perhaps it was time for this conversation. Rafael's sister was her baby nephew's temporary legal guardian. After Arielle had died, Eve came to Royal to reunite Micah with his father. Only, she fell sick and was hospitalized within hours of her arrival, leaving her baby nephew in need of care. Cammie Wentworth, by virtue of being in the right place at the right time, had offered to foster him.

"It's sort of awkward meeting you like this," Eve said. "Your sister is my nephew's guardian."

"Ah!" he said. "I was wondering who that little kid was."

Eve saw right through him. No amount of humor would make this less awkward. "Your sister is a very good person. She's been a lifesaver."

He looked at her steadily. "She's the best. I'm the problem child."

"I can see that."

"Cammie and I didn't grow up together," he explained. "What came between you and your sister?"

"There was the age difference between us. It wasn't that great, but add to that a stark difference in personality. We were always competing with each other."

"For guys?"

"Ugh!" Eve groaned. "Only a guy would think that."

Rafael bowed slightly. "I apologize for dumb guys everywhere."

"We competed for everything except guys," Eve said. "Arielle was a butterfly, drifting from adventure to adventure. She thought I was a bore. You can say we led competing lifestyles."

"You…a bore? Where did she get that?"

"She wrote it in her diary."

"She wrote 'Eve is a bore' in her diary?"

"Not those exact words," Eve said.

Arielle was a crafty writer. Her exact words: *If only Eve could get out of her own way, get some new friends, get away for a weekend, get laid, get a job she actually likes. Sheesh!*

"I think you're plenty fun."

"Just wait until I bore you to tears with my lists and spreadsheets."

"You're organized," he said. "I can appreciate that."

"Well, my sister couldn't. It drove her crazy."

"Sounds like classic sibling rivalry," he said. "Family isn't always the best judge of things, Eve. I can tell you that."

"More than petty rivalry," Eve said. "We were hell-bent on proving the other wrong. I wanted her to see that my orderly way of life was the best, the most secure. And it kills me because, in the end, when she returned home from Texas, pregnant, scared and ashamed, the way she looked at me…" Eve's throat tightened. "I could tell she thought I'd won." Eve's voice cracked. She paused to take a breath. "I didn't win, you know? I didn't win a damn thing."

"No one wins this stupid game," Rafael said quietly. "No one."

"Well, I lost big time," Eve said. "After giving birth, my sister had some…heart problems. Meanwhile, I had my own problems. Things were a mess at work and soon after she died, I lost my job under a hailstorm of false accusations of fraud. My face was on the local news and my accounts were frozen. It was hell. The lawyers doubted the court would let me keep Micah. So I hopped on the first bus to Texas, collapsed, ended up in the hospital bed and lost Micah, anyway."

"And that's when Cammie stepped in?" he asked.

Eve looked down at her hands.

Rafael let out a low whistle. "That's a lot."

Eve agreed. It was a whole helluva lot. She hadn't even shared the most harrowing details. After meeting with the lawyer and faced with the prospect of losing custody of Micah, Eve had sat sobbing in her car for an hour before hatching the plan to flee west. It was imperative she reunite Micah with his father. What choice did she have? She was facing possible criminal indictment. If it turned out that she wasn't free to raise him, she had to make sure he was left in good hands. Unfortunately, she couldn't just call the man. Arielle had never shared his identity, and Eve had not wanted to pry. Then her sister had died suddenly and it was too late.

That afternoon, she drove home and, heart pounding, started to pack. She tossed her clothes and important papers into a suitcase and grabbed the tin with the ten grand in cash that she'd inherited from her grandmother. She stuffed Micah's diaper bag with packets of formula, diapers and a dozen onesies. As she'd packed the bag, she found the most important thing hidden in a side pocket: a diary that Arielle had left behind. It detailed her time in Royal. It likely held the only clues Eve would ever have to discover the identity of Micah's father. When she was about ready to leave, she sat with the baby to collect herself and cried some more. It had been the worst night of her life.

"So, you see," she said. "I don't blame you for being upset where my sister is concerned. I know how it feels to be falsely accused of something. It's terrible, and no one should have to go through that."

He studied her awhile. "A simple paternity test cleared my name. It wasn't quite so easy for you. What happened there?"

"Don't you know?" How she'd lost her dream job under criminal allegations was a part of her past that she'd rather not think about, let alone discuss with a stranger over tequila.

"I might have heard a few rumors."

"Allegedly, I embezzled hundreds of thousands of dollars from the financial firm that gave me my start."

Rafael refilled his glass. "Stealing from a greedy investment banker isn't really stealing, is it?"

"Stealing is stealing."

"Alright," he said dismissively. "But you didn't steal anything."

Eve raised her chin, defiant. "How do you know?"

"You're not that clever."

Ouch! That stung. Eve couldn't even hide it. "I was pretty good at my job."

"Am I wrong?" he asked.

"Dead wrong," she fired back. "It wasn't a complicated scheme! I could've come up with it."

"Maybe," he said coolly. "But you couldn't have executed it."

"I can do whatever I put my mind to."

In the back of her mind, Eve knew her outrage was misplaced. He was, in a strange way, taking her off the hook. Why was she so desperate to hang on?

"Sorry to take a swipe at your criminal credentials," he said. "But you nearly passed out at the thought of tipping over a champagne tower at a country club. You really want me to believe you embezzled money from one of Miami's most powerful financiers?"

Well…he had her there. "In any case, they caught the person who tried to frame me. I'm in the clear."

"All's well that ends well," he said with a crooked smile.

He picked a wedge of lime from the bowl and brought it to his lips. Eve watched, transfixed, and once again fell straight through the trapdoor of her imagination. She was in the lobby again, kissing him. For all his talk about his grandmother, Rafael was not the type of guy you brought home to meet your own grandma. He was good for making a woman *feel* good. And there he sat at arm's reach, unguarded and practically undressed. Eve could *never* embezzle hundreds of thousands of dollars, not from a greedy financier or anyone. But maybe, just maybe, she could pull this off.

Eve rose to her knees and loosened the knot of her robe.

Rafael set down his glass on the coffee table with a definitive tap. "What are you doing?"

"I'm letting my guard down."

The sides of the robe fell open. His heated gaze raked her body. "Eve..." he said. "What did I say about that?"

She was far from caring. "I want the night you promised."

He leaned his head back against the seat of the chair, watching her through narrowed eyes. "Pretty sure I didn't promise this."

Eve drew her robe shut. "My mistake then."

Before she could tie the belt, he caught it and tugged her to him. She fell forward into his arms. The kiss in the lobby had been the slow, getting-to-know-you sort. By now, though, they knew each other just fine, and this kiss was rough and demanding. His hands roamed her body. Eve tried to straddle him, but he eased her away. "Eve, we have a dilemma."

"What's that?"

"Either we call our man downstairs and ask him to send up a box of condoms or—"

She silenced him, first with a finger to his lips then with her mouth pressed to his. "Just kiss me."

With adept hands, he pushed the heavy robe off her shoulders. Then he eased her away again and took in her naked body. "Where?"

"Wherever you like."

He lowered her onto the floor and pressed a kiss in the dip at the base of her neck. "Where else? Show me."

Eve pointed to her navel and he followed her fingertips with his lips. Next, she guided him to her hip. Slowly, methodically, he pressed hot kisses all over her aching body. His tenderness and care soothed her aching heart. Eve twisted and arched her back, doing whatever necessary to meet his mouth wherever it wandered.

Kissing on the lush carpet: exquisite.

Six

Eve curled up in bed. She dreamed of Rafael's fingers grazing her skin, soft laughter in the dark and kisses pressed into her eager body. She dreamed of coming so close to pleasure only to be denied, again and again, until the denial was its own pleasure. Then she woke up shivering and alone—not just in bed, but the hotel suite. She called out to Rafael, and the only response was silence. There was a note on the bedside table. She read it twice, still a little hungover from all that tequila.

Eve, sweet, something's come up. I have to go, but I don't have the heart to wake you. A few things:
    Your dress is in the hall closet.
    Call room service and breakfast will be delivered.
    When you're ready to go, contact the con-

cierge. A car is waiting to take you home or any-
where you need to go.
   Everything is taken care of.
   Here's my cell number. 954-333-1100
Call me.
—R.

So...he'd bolted. Maybe he wasn't such a good guy, after all. Was it any surprise, really? This must be his MO, abandoning women in hotel rooms, sneaking out while they slept. She wouldn't have pegged him for that sort of guy. For whatever reason, the idea didn't take root. She wanted to give him the benefit of the doubt.

Eve climbed out of bed. On the bright side, she did have an entire suite to herself. Last week, she'd moved out of her Airbnb host's guest bedroom into their renovated detached garage. She had more privacy, but not much more space. Here, she had so much space she could do cartwheels—although her physical therapist would not approve.

Eve called for room service. The order had already been placed, and within fifteen minutes the food was delivered. Say what you like about the Belleview Inn, the service was prompt. There was a bit of everything, mostly healthy options like oatmeal, yogurt and fruit, but also bacon—crispy, crunchy, salty, tasty bacon. She reached for a strip then dropped it. Her life was oatmeal. No bacon, no more steak or liquor, and no escapades with sexy strangers allowed. She poured herself a glass of orange juice and wandered the connected rooms. Everything looked different in the morning light. Eve took in the pale yellow wallpaper, thick maroon drapes, heavy wood furniture and framed paintings of horses. *Decor: traditional to a fault.*

The bed in the second bedroom was pristine. Rafael had slept with her last night, and the bed they'd shared was a crime scene. He'd kissed her everywhere then scooped her into his arms and carried her to bed. They fell asleep, limbs intertwined, skin-to-skin. It took all Eve's willpower to keep from climbing back into that bed and under the sheets just to feel him again. But she couldn't indulge in this fantasy. She'd had her fun; it was time to get back to reality.

After breakfast, Eve poured herself a bath and tossed a floral-scented bath bomb into the warm water. She had to wash Rafael Wentworth's scent off her body. Where best to do it than in a claw-foot tub?

When Eve finally made it home, she pulled on a pair of pink leggings and a matching top, holdovers from her hot yoga days. She had a physical therapy session later that afternoon, and for once she was looking forward to it. It seemed she couldn't sit still one minute without feeling Rafael's lips tracing circles on her breasts. If she shut her eyes, even briefly, his phone number blinked in the back of her mind like a neon sign.

She had to forget the happy-go-lucky Rafael Wentworth. They were too different. Tonight, while he'd likely meet with friends for dinner, she'd eat ramen in bed while applying for random jobs online. She was fine with it. Eve was no longer interested in comparing her life to anyone else's. This was what she had to do to stay afloat. Her focus was on building a secure future for herself and her little nephew.

She sent a text message to Cammie, her nephew's

benefactor, for lack of a better word. She wanted to visit before therapy. Holding the baby would help her reconnect with her priorities.

Eve's love for Micah was tethered with guilt. There was nothing she could do to sever the two emotions. It had been that way ever since the nurse had placed her newborn nephew in her arms. Arielle was not well, and the infant needed skin-to-skin contact. The joy of new life coupled with anxiety over her sister's declining health had overwhelmed Eve. She held Micah close and sang to him, just like her grandmother had sung to her. Skin-to-skin contact: the fabric of family.

Arielle wasn't well, but no one had expected her to die. The heart attack that took her life three weeks after Micah's birth had even shocked her doctors. Yet unexpected death and soul-wrenching heartache was the one thing life had prepared Eve for. She'd lost her parents in a fatal accident not too long ago. All that being said, she would not lose Micah. She refused.

Micah was her heart. She would move heaven and earth to ensure he had the future that he deserved. She hadn't come to Royal to have fun or flirt with gorgeous men. She had one specific task: track down Micah's father. According to Arielle's diary, he was a TCC member. A DNA test had ruled out Rafael, but that left a sizable portion of Royal's wealthy male population. Unfortunately, that was the only clue she had.

Eve touched the hollow of her neck, the very spot where Rafael had planted a kiss. She'd keep the memory alive, but resolved to shelf the man away for good. She could handle only one life-shattering event at a time. Given the opportunity, Rafael Wentworth would shatter her heart. She knew his type. His rushing off this morning had made it all the more clear. He was not one to get attached. When he was ready to move on, he'd leave a big, gaping wound in her life for her to stitch up on her own. Eve had nursed enough wounds, both physically and emotionally, and would not survive another.

Her mind made up, she grabbed her keys and her bus pass and set out for the day.

Seven

It had killed Rafael to leave that note for Eve, but his options were limited. A 4:00 a.m. phone call got him out of bed. The news hadn't been good. Scaffolding at the construction site of his newly acquired property had collapsed. The luxe guest ranch was still under construction and not yet open to clients. The main house with reception, offices and a few permanent suites was complete. The restaurant was half-finished, and his Michelin-starred chef was busy creating new recipes and testing them on the staff. Rafael hoped to have everything up and running in six months. It would be tight, but doable. But that meant overseeing everything himself.

Eve was in deep sleep, her face soft. He didn't have it in him to wake her.

Like a thief, he'd crept out of the suite, stopping at

the front desk to make the necessary arrangements. On the drive to the site, he worried as much about the accident as he did about her waking up alone and confused at the Belleview Inn. Eve and her air of mystery. Eve and her scandalous past. Eve and her uncertain future. Eve with skin like caramel.

Weeks ago, Cammie had wanted to introduce him to her protégé of sorts, thinking that two outsiders from Florida might hit it off. His sister wasn't wrong, but he and Eve had more than Miami in common. They were outsiders in every sense of the word. Rafael even understood her reasons for dressing up and heading out last night. It was his preferred way of coping with life's ups and downs, a method he'd perfected over the years. He knew how isolating it could feel to be the odd one out in this tightly knit community, and he wasn't going to let her twist all alone in the wind.

He intended to call her as soon as he got a chance. With all the chaos on the construction site, the opportunity didn't present itself until midmorning. It was too late. The Belleview Inn front desk clerk informed him that his guest had checked out an hour ago.

He took a break around noon and drove out to the car shop to finalize the purchase of the Camaro. The location was just as odd looking in the daylight as it had been the night before. A gravel path led to the concrete block of a building. The blinking neon OPEN sign over the metal door was the only indicator that it was a place of business, and not home base for a garage band. Manny clasped him on the shoulder. "Good thing you left your top hat and tails at home this time. You can join us for lunch."

With the accident at the construction site, Rafael hadn't bothered to dress for work. He'd stopped by the residence, slipped on a black T-shirt, jeans and a pair of boots. Manny wore a denim button-down shirt and cargo pants. They were roughly the same age and both successful in their own right. Manny had worked in one of the most prestigious shops in Dallas before relocating to his hometown of Royal.

Inside the "showroom," several cars were lined up. The Camaro was draped with a canvas cloth.

"I'm excited for you, man," Manny said. "Want another look?"

"What do you think?"

With a yank, Manny revealed what looked like a carcass of a car dragged up from a swamp. Rafael winced, hit with buyer's remorse. The harsh light of day revealed cracks and dents he might have overlooked the night before. What on the mother-loving earth had he agreed to purchase?

"Hey! Show some respect," Manny said. "This is a 1969 Camaro—"

"No, it's not," Rafael interrupted. "That's what it used to be."

"Once upon a time this beast tore up the asphalt."

"No doubt. But *today* it's a rotting tin can."

"Having second thoughts? It happens. You gotta have faith, bro," Manny said. "If you can't see the beauty in this, I can't help you."

Rafael considered the curved contours of the car's rusted body. He saw the beauty. He wasn't willing to admit it, though.

"When I'm done with this tin can, it'll fetch north of five hundred grand at auction. So you can get in on it now for the low, low price that we agreed on last night or you can drive off in your pretty car and have a nice life."

"What's your plan for the engine?" Rafael asked. No amount of trash talk was going to throw him off.

After a lengthy discussion, Rafael tossed the pen he'd used to sign the papers at Manny, aiming for his head. The next thing Rafael knew, they were seated at a round table in the back of the garage, eating barbecue with a pair of mechanics and talking about cars. It was a welcome distraction. He worried about Eve, wondered if she'd gotten home alright. And why hadn't she called him? He didn't have her number, and with no way to reach her, he was at a loss.

After lunch, Rafael drove slowly along the busy streets. She lived in this part of town, didn't she? Too bad he hadn't memorized her address. He considered asking around. She was such a polarizing figure in Royal that he could likely get her address from anyone on the street. Or…he could ask his peach of a sister. The idea struck him between the eyes. Eve's nephew was in Cammie's care, his darling sister's care. Damn it! He should have thought of it hours ago.

Rafael pressed hard on the gas. Twenty minutes later, he pulled up to Drake and Cammie's ranch. Drake was Micah's official foster parent and Cammie was the primary caregiver. Or did he have that wrong? It hadn't occurred to him to ask before. It was a temporary arrangement, and complicated, too. His sister wanted children; she'd always been clear about that. Drake, though, had preferred his freedom. Honestly, Rafael couldn't blame him. However, by taking in Micah and helping Cammie through this time, Drake seemed to be coming around.

Rafael was mulling this over when Drake approached and tapped on his windshield, peering at him with his ice-blue eyes. Rafael climbed out of the car.

"Rafe! You're early, man," Drake said good-humoredly.

Rafael had started visiting Cammie on Friday afternoons. It was his attempt to meet his sister halfway. They were starting over. Cammie was just a kid back when he'd moved in with his father and teenage Rafe wanted nothing to do with her. The children of dysfunction, they had no prior relationship to fall back on, no well of childhood memories to draw from in bad times. Rafael had left his father's house at seventeen when it was clear he had no place in the Wentworth clan. His very existence was a black mark to the Wentworth name. When he left for Florida, he vowed never to return.

Cammie had reached out to him constantly over the years, then she started writing letters advocating on their father's behalf. Losing his third wife, the love of his life, had wrecked him. Apparently, he'd changed. The old man then reached out, pleading for another chance. It was time to stop ignoring them. And here Rafael was, back in Texas, far from the life he had built for himself and second-guessing his decision every day. However, he was committed to repairing his relationship with his father and would remain in Royal for as long as it took. He'd taken on projects to justify staying in town, even just to himself. The guest ranch and the Camaro were necessary tools. The projects kept him moving at a fast pace while he took on the slow work of getting to know his estranged father and becoming the brother Cammie deserved. He felt certain that this was something that he had to work through. His anger toward his family had served as armor. As a teen, he'd needed that extra protection. But as an adult, it only weighed him down.

Rafael had taken some measures, baby steps, really, to reconnect with his family. On Saturdays, he met his father for lunch, usually at the TCC's Colt Room. On Fridays, he visited with Cammie. They'd sit outside with coffee and talk. It had been awkward at first. He was the reason her family had blown up. Her mother left their father after he finally came around to acknowledging Rafael as his son. And yet, Cammie didn't resent him. He doubted he'd be so generous if it were the other way around.

He and Drake headed toward the house.

"Cammie is inside with Eve and the baby," Drake said. "Want to grab a beer?"

Rafael slowed to a stop. "What did you say?"

"Beer. Want to grab one?"

That wasn't the answer Rafael was looking for. He said yes to the beer and, heart pounding, dashed ahead of Drake up the front steps. He'd cleared the door when he realized that Drake had meant for them to grab a beer while Cammie visited with Eve. Well, too bad and too late for that. He followed the sound of voices into the kitchen. There she was at the kitchen table in pink leggings, hair in a floppy ponytail, golden brown skin flushed, no makeup and no lipstick to wipe away with a kiss. His heart fell into a ditch. *There you are, sugar plum.*

Cammie was at the stove stirring a pot. "Hey, you! I wasn't expecting you this early."

"I was in the neighborhood and thought I'd stop by and say hi." He sought Eve's eyes. "Hello, Eve."

"You just happened to be in this neighborhood?" Drake said.

"And how do you two know each other?" Cammie said.

Eve looked a little panicked. She cradled Micah in her arms.

"Everyone knows everyone in this two-horse town," Rafael said, teasing his sister and throwing her off their scent.

"Whatever!" Cammie fired back. "I'm glad you two have met. You've got a lot in common."

"So you keep saying."

Drake slapped him on the shoulder and handed him the beer that he'd forgotten about. "Don't stare," he whispered. "You'll scare her."

He couldn't help but stare. The woman before him now, soft, tender, unhurried, cradling a baby in her arms, was the same person he'd met last night, sharp, direct, bemoaning her former "30 Under 30" status. He had to wrap his head around that.

Eve's phone buzzed and she slipped it out of an invisible pocket of her body-hugging leggings. One glance at the screen and she let out a groan.

"What is it?" Cammie said.

"My therapist has to reschedule."

"You're in therapy?" Rafael said.

"Physical therapy," she replied without looking at him. "I'm still wobbly on my feet."

Last night he'd assumed that her heels were the problem. He knew about her long hospital stay. Even so, he hadn't suspected a physical impairment. Guilt wormed through him. He'd kept her up and fed her steak and dowsed her with tequila and made her body twist to his will. Just how oblivious was he?

"Are you okay?" he asked.

"I'm fine!" She followed that declaration with a look that said: *You know I'm fine!*

Rafael shook his head. He knew no such thing.

Her phone buzzed again. She looked at her nephew and made a decision. "Take him, please," she told Rafael. "I have to answer this. They need me to reschedule."

He went over to where she sat and lifted the baby from her lap. While she typed on her phone, he took in Micah with new eyes. He had a head of black curls and was as plump and golden brown as a loaf of bread. Micah stared at him with skepticism. He had Eve's eyes. Rafael tickled his chin to find out if he had Eve's smile, as well. Micah did not smile. Solid little kid.

"Look how good you are with him!" Cammie exclaimed. "Remember that first time? You wouldn't even touch him."

"I remember." Babies were cute and all, just not for him.

"You'll make a great dad someday."

Rafael raised an eyebrow. "Have you seen the cars I drive? There's no room for baby seats."

"You'll upgrade to a family sedan." It was as if she'd had his whole future mapped out.

Drake leaned against the counter. "Or get a truck like the rest of us."

Rafael was going to hurl up his beer. Now was probably not the time to bring up his expensive new purchase.

Eve returned. "I'll take him now." She waited as Rafael placed Micah back on her lap.

Drake spoke up. "Heard there was an accident on your property."

Rafael had forgotten how quickly word traveled in Royal. "Scaffolding collapsed on the site."

Cammie had abandoned the pot and worked a knife through a stash of herbs. "Was anyone hurt?"

He locked eyes with Eve. "No, but it dragged me out of bed at four in the morning."

"You couldn't have been happy about that," Drake said.

"God, I hated it," Rafael said. "You have no idea what it cost me."

Eve turned away, her cheeks the color of wine.

"You can't be everywhere at once," Cammie said. "You need help."

"I'm looking to hire an assistant."

"Don't you already have one?" Cammie asked.

His sister had visited the property and met his staff. "You mean Dan? He's overseeing HR and general management stuff. I need someone more detail-oriented for daily operations."

"We've used a local recruitment firm," Cammie said. "Remind me to get you the number."

"Sure," he said, already forgetting all about it. Eve was giving him a hard look, even as she bounced Micah lightly on her lap to the baby's delight. What was she trying to tell him? Her phone buzzed again and stole her focus. He nearly groaned in frustration. When had he become so needy? He needed to know what she'd wanted to say. On top of that, he needed to know why she hadn't called. And it didn't stop there. He needed to know more about her physical therapy and the nature of her injuries, if any. He needed to know if she had dinner plans. If she didn't, would she agree to grab a bite with him?

"Oh, no!" Eve cried. "They want me to come in *now*."

"What's wrong with now?" Cammie asked. She sprinkled the chopped herbs into whatever it was she was cooking. And whatever it was, it smelled really good. "Take my car. I'm not going anywhere."

Rafael had assumed that Eve had chosen not to drive last night, but that didn't seem to be the case. She didn't have a car, here, in Royal, Texas, where public transportation was a sort of practical joke the local government played on its people.

"I can take you," he said.

Out of the corner of his eye, Rafael caught Drake laughing into his beer bottle.

"Big bro to the rescue!" Cammie cried. "It's settled. Rafe will take you."

God, he loved his sister.

"No, thanks," Eve said, hugging Micah to her chest. The little boy reached up and dug his chubby fingers into her cheek. "I don't want to impose."

"It's no trouble," Rafael said.

Nothing she could ask of him would be too much. He would drive across this state and back if she needed him to. He wasn't sure his hard stare could convey all of that, but he put in the effort.

Eve hesitated a moment. "Okay."

"It's settled," Cammie said. "Now go on, you two."

Eve held up Micah and spoke to him. "Auntie Evie has to go to therapy now. Remember I told you about therapy? I'd love to stay and give you a bath and read you a story. Next time. Okay?"

Rafael watched as she planted a kiss on Micah's forehead and whispered a secret in his ear. A wave of tenderness crashed into him.

Cammie took Micah from her. "Don't worry about it. We've got bath time covered."

His little sister was the most generous, bighearted person Rafael knew. She loved children. It made sense that Eve would entrust Micah to her.

Drake ushered them out the door. "Go on. Don't get into trouble."

Rafael and Eve walked to the car in silence, each aware they were being watched.

"Thanks for the ride," she said.

"Were you ever going to call?" he asked.

"No."

"Why?"

"Not important."

Like hell it wasn't. "You thought I skipped out on you?"

"Yes and no."

He held open the car door for her. "You're not making sense."

"Don't worry, I'm over it." She climbed in. "There's something else I want to talk to you about."

Really? He could think of literally nothing else he wanted to talk about. The minute he joined her in the car, she grabbed his arm, digging her nails in his biceps. He welcomed the contact, but questioned her motives. "What's up?"

"Hire me!"

"What?"

"You need an assistant and I need a job. Hire me!"

So, that's what it was all about, Rafael thought, driving off Drake's property. She wanted the executive assistant job.

"You'll never find anyone more detail-oriented than me," she said. "I'll learn the business. I'll do whatever it takes."

Rafael stopped at a light. "You got the job."

She released his arm. "Well…don't do me any favors. You should go through your regular process."

"You're of two minds on everything, Eve. Anyone ever tell you that?"

"I'm a Gemini," she said. "I'm not asking for a handout. All I ask is that you consider my application."

"How about an interview?" he suggested. "Would that make you feel better?"

"Yes, it would," she said. "Then you can judge for yourself whether or not I meet your needs."

Rafael suppressed a laugh. She met his needs, and she damn well knew it.

"Where are we headed?" he asked.

"Wait a minute."

She pulled out her phone and tapped an app for directions. She was the most app-dependent person he knew. "You really don't know your way around, do you?"

She clutched the phone. "It won't impact my job performance. I rely on GPS, sure, but I always find my way around."

"Settle down, Eve," he said. "The interview isn't until later."

If anything, she was overqualified with her extensive experience in finance. And last night had taught him one thing: they made a great team.

"Later when?" she asked.

"How about tonight?" he proposed.

"Is that when you usually interview candidates? At night?"

Her clipped tone cut him. He resented the implication. "It is, actually," he said. "I take the top two candidates out for dinner. I only hire people I'm comfortable with. My business is my life."

Her expression fell. "Oh."

Rafael's hands tightened on the wheel. He understood all that he was giving up to offer her this job. As his employee, she would be off-limits. He'd have to forget everything that had happened the night before and wasn't sure he could. Was it too late to take back the offer and help her find some other job? Maybe at his father's nonprofit?

They arrived at the therapy clinic. Rafael found a parking spot in a shady area of the lot, but Eve had only minutes to spare before her appointment.

"Today we're doing lower body strength training," she said. "Woo-hoo!"

He released his seat belt and faced her. "Why do you need therapy?"

"I was in the hospital awhile and it's like they say— use it or lose it."

"Why were you in the hospital?"

"Haven't you heard?"

No use pretending he hadn't heard the gossip. "They say you collapsed and fell unconscious. No one ever says why."

"It's too much to get into right now," she said. "And I promise I'm getting better. It won't affect my job performance."

"Oh, God, Eve... Enough with that."

She averted her eyes, looking out the car window at the bland outpatient clinic. "Sorry. I'm just anxious."

He reached for her hand, but thought better of it. "I understand."

"I have to go," she said. "They'll cancel my appointment if I'm late."

"How are you getting home?" he asked.

"Don't worry. I can manage."

"Manage how?"

"There's a shuttle bus for patients."

"It takes you to your door?"

"It takes me close enough and the walk is good exercise."

"I can wait here until you're done."

"Don't even think about it." She opened the car door. Before stepping out, she leaned in as if to kiss him and then stopped short. Had it finally clicked? He was no longer her potential lover. He was her future boss. Regret pooled in her brown eyes. She blinked and pulled away from him. "So, about that interview. Time? Place?"

"Tomorrow morning at nine. Does that work?"

"It works."

"Text me and I'll send you the address," he said. "You still have my number, right?"

That simple question brought back the note and the events of the night before that she refused to acknowledge. "Yeah. I have your number," she said, and slipped out of his reach.

Eight

Eve had her mind on her money. If she had to choose between good sex and a good job, she was going for the job. No doubt about it. Too bad the same man had the power to offer both. No, that wasn't quite true. He was offering one or the other, and she had made her choice. She'd seen the disappointment in his eyes. It mirrored her own. No one would ever hold her like he had, press kisses into her skin, whisper her name, tease her, tug her hair...

Eve's fingers trembled when she texted him a short, brief message later that night. This is Eve.

I'm sorry. Who?

She sent him an eye roll emoji. He sent her a photo of him biting into a monster burger. The message read: This is dinner.

She snapped a photo of her cup of low-sodium noodles and sent it along.

His response came quickly. Toss that out and come join me. I'll treat you to Royal's best veggie burger.

She took her phone and cup of noodles to bed. Nope! Sorry. I have a big interview in the morning with a certain Mr. Wentworth.

You have an interview with a certain Mr. Arias. And brace yourself, I hear he's a jerk.

Arias? Really?

If local gossip held a kernel of truth, his mother, Rosa Arias, was a local girl of Mexican descent. Tobias Wentworth got his mistress pregnant but had no intention of ever marrying her.

Arias. Really. Haven't you heard? I'm the big, bad, black sheep.

A wicked smile tugged at her lips. A wolf in black sheep's clothing is what you are.

He responded with a wolf emoji. Be careful. Don't get lost in the woods.

She tapped her thumb against the screen wondering what to reply next. Thankfully, he sent her the address and wished her good-night. Eve fell breathless onto her pillow. She should crave safety, but she didn't.

Earlier today, when Rafael had stormed into Cammie's kitchen as if it were the beaches of Normandy, her heart had tanked. She visited often and had never run into him in the past. Besides, he'd said they weren't close. In Drake and Cammie's kitchen, drinking beer straight from the bottle, he was not the perfectly put together man she'd met the night before. The country club member. An heir to the Wentworth fortune. Scruffy, unshaven, tousled hair, wrinkled T-shirt, plain jeans, and even a little grease under his fingernails. She could barely look at him for wanting him so much.

That night Eve went to bed early, but she did not sleep a wink.

Her alarm rang at six thirty on the dot. It took her a while to find an interview-appropriate outfit. Normally, this wouldn't be a problem. She had been dressing for the job she wanted instead of the sucky job she had ever since she was old enough to vote. Too bad she had left her collection of pantsuits back in Miami. For her interview with "Mr. Arias," she settled on a blue silk blouse, a navy pencil skirt and a pair of pumps.

Eve left her place with plenty of time to arrive at the guest ranch and freshen up in the restroom before the 9:00 a.m. interview. Unfortunately, she hadn't planned for the delays. The bus arrived twenty minutes late and broke down a few blocks from the appointed address. Rather than sit and wait for a new one to arrive, Eve hopped out and walked the rest of the way.

The Arias property sat on an impressive spread of land. From the guard gate, a long driveway to the main house extended under a canopy of leafy trees. It was 9:05. She was officially late.

This was not the first impression Eve had wanted to make. Her goal was to force him to see her as more than a charity case. Showing up sweaty and exhausted at a morning interview wasn't the way to go about it.

She ambled along the cobblestone walkway in her sensible heels. Her feet hurt. When she thought of the way she used to strut in stilettos along the crowded sidewalks of Miami's financial district with a cup of Starbucks in one hand and her phone pressed to her ear, it made her want to cry. As it was, she couldn't even safely carry her nephew until she built up adequate upper body strength. The rehab doctors had prohibited it.

Eve arrived at the main house and limped into the reception area. She breathed in the chilled air and soaked in her surroundings. The decor was minimal and modern, all tall windows, cream upholstery and cognac leather.

First impression: wow!

A receptionist looked up from a computer monitor. "Are you Eve Martin?"

"Yes." Eve stepped forward. "I know I'm late."

"Just by a few minutes." The young blonde woman rose from behind a smooth, curved marble desk. "What happened to you? Did you cross a desert to get here?"

Eve could die of embarrassment. "The bus broke down."

"Yikes!" The receptionist offered her a bottle of water. "Let's get you fixed up."

"But I'm late," Eve stammered.

"Exactly. What's five more minutes?" Her message was clear: better to show up fashionably late, than sweaty and on time. "I'm Audrey, by the way."

"Nice to meet you, Audrey."

From behind the desk she produced a pack of tissues, face mist and a compact mirror. "Here you go."

Audrey was young, barely twenty, and had all the can-do spirit that came with that age. "Don't mention it. I was super nervous when I interviewed with the great Rafael Arias Wentworth. Seriously, though, he is amazing and this is the best place I've ever worked. Seeing what you went through to get here, you must really want this job."

From the mountaintop of legal and medical bills where she was perched, Eve saw things differently. She desperately needed this job. She was living off meager savings and the modest inheritance from her grandmother.

Eve checked her reflection in the mirror and smoothed back her hair. She wore it in her signature bun at the nape of her neck. She blotted her face and reapplied lipstick. One spray of mint-scented mist and she was ready.

"Much better," Audrey said. "I'll let Mr. Arias Wentworth know you're here."

Mr. Arias Wentworth. That was a mouthful. Would she have to call him that? Would he call her Ms. Martin? How awkward would that be? She'd spooned with this man.

"Take the stairs or the elevator to the second floor," Audrey said, giving her one last push. "Good luck!"

Eve took the elevator, which turned out to be a mistake. It took her right back to the elevator at the Belleview Inn and that first real, heartfelt conversation they'd had. That took her back to the first kiss they'd shared in the inn's lobby. And that looped her back to the time he'd pushed off her robe and lowered her onto the carpeted floor. Her cheeks were burning when the elevator doors slid open. There stood Rafael Arias Wentworth, laid-back yet professional in a tailored blue blazer paired with a sky blue button-down shirt. His dark hair was slightly wet and brushed neatly. This was corporate casual Rafael, and she wanted to yank him into the elevator and leave lipstick stains on his crisp collar. Their eyes met, and she had no doubt he knew exactly what she was thinking.

This was getting off to a great start.

Nine

Rafael greeted her when she stepped out of the elevator. "Good morning," he said. "I was about to give up on you."

Eve didn't believe him. He would never give up on her. That type of certainty was odd this early in any relationship. "Sorry I'm late. It won't happen again."

"No worries," he said. "Come with me."

He led her past the deserted reception area to his office suite tucked behind a pair of frosted glass doors. His name was etched on the glass in straightforward print: Rafael Arias Wentworth.

"Take what you need and drop that heavy purse here," he said, pointing to a smooth suede couch.

"We're not doing it here?" she asked, rummaging through her purse for the mini tablet with her résumé. She didn't have a hard copy. The print shop was closed by the time she'd made it out of physical therapy.

"No, we're not," he said. "Let's go. Breakfast is waiting."

Breakfast! Her mood took off on a hot-air balloon. She'd munched on a cereal bar on the bus and now she was starving.

Rafael led her out of the office suite and took the stairs to the lobby. Eve had no choice but to follow. The stairs were steep, and the glossy marble tile looked slippery. She clung to the rail like a toddler. Her therapy diagnoses were disturbing: *abnormality of gait, general muscle weakness, and lack of coordination.* The goal was to regain her "prior level of function." Because she had yet to do so, the social worker on the case had marked her as unfit to care for an infant or child full time. With each session, Eve was getting stronger. Her endurance and balance had greatly improved. Still, uneven surfaces remained a challenge. She was working with her therapist on that, too.

Audrey smiled up at them from the reception desk. When Rafael wasn't looking, she gave Eve the good old thumbs-up. Eve cringed. She had no idea how much of her self-confidence was tied with her physical well-being. She'd always been athletic and capable, playing sports through high school and, in recent years, keeping up her fitness with rigorous gym classes. And here she was, clinging to a handrail, taking careful steps, while Rafael took confident long strides. When he reached the landing, she'd only made it halfway down. He swiveled around and raced back up, taking the stairs by twos.

"I'm sorry," he said when he reached her. "I should be more careful with you."

"No, you shouldn't," she said through clenched teeth.

"Yes, I should," Rafael insisted. "What's wrong with that?"

Nothing. Absolutely nothing was wrong with it, except that it made her feel weak and pathetic. This last year had revealed her greatest flaw: an inability to accept help of any kind with any sort of grace.

Rafael would not budge. He offered his arm and waited for her to take it. Reluctantly, she looped a hand around his elbow. To touch him again, even like this, made her flinch. Together, they made it down the stairs. He led her out of the building through a wide door made of reclaimed wood. The vast property sloped west, and he pointed out the limits beyond a tuft of pine trees. A gazebo was set up with a round dining table. Rafael held out her chair and told her the chef was working out the kinks in the new kitchen. To keep things simple, he'd requested one dish: a Spanish omelet. "No sausage. No bacon."

"Thanks for that."

Rafael plucked a croissant from a basket at the center of the table. "You wouldn't meet with me for dinner, so I got creative."

Eve handed him the iPad opened to her résumé. He took it from her and set it aside. "There'll be time enough for that," he said. "How was your night?"

"Mr. Arias Wentworth," Eve said, "I can't tell you how to do your job, but you should start with the standard interview questions. Like… What are your strengths? Or… Where do you see yourself in five years?"

"What *are* your strengths?" he asked.

"Um…" She was distracted by the way he toyed with

a butter knife. She imagined reaching across the table and mingling her trembling fingers with his strong ones.

"And tell me your weaknesses, while you're at it."

"I'm practical," she replied. "I have no trouble setting aside fantasy to focus on reality."

Rafael flashed a half smile. "That's not the standard answer."

"Alright." She tried again. "I'm stubborn. I won't give up on a problem until it's solved."

"That's more like it," he said, and slid the iPad across the table. "Why not just tell me what's here?"

"Sure," Eve said, suddenly nervous. She might have to peek at her own résumé to get the facts straight. "I attended FIU, both for undergrad and business school. Then I accepted an internship with the firm and gradually worked my way up."

He nodded his approval. "Very good."

"You know how the story ends, so it wasn't all that good."

Rafael tilted his head, studying her. Eve knew what he was thinking. She was the one to continually bring up the scandal—not him, not anyone, just her. Even when offered a fresh start, all she could do was dig up the relics of the past.

Rafael picked up the pot of coffee from the center of the table and poured her a cup. "Sugar?"

"Please."

He added two cubes to her cup and presented it to her like a gift. Her hand trembled as she took it from his hand to her lips.

"You may be overqualified for the job that I originally had in mind."

Eve shrugged. "It's this or bus tables, so…"

"Not true," he said. "You have options. Between Cammie, Drake and I, we can find you a job."

"No." Eve set down her coffee cup. She didn't want to work anywhere else.

"Audrey says this is a great place to work and you're a dream boss."

"Gotta love Audrey!" Rafael said with a low laugh. "Though I wish that were the case, it's not. I'm not a dream anything. I can be difficult, Eve."

"How so?" she asked, wondering who was sitting across the table from her this morning. Was it the black sheep or the gray wolf?

"I'm going through some things," he said. "Coming back to Royal, dealing with Tobias, getting to know Cammie… It's been hard."

She could only imagine. Rafael had inherited a mix bag of snacks: money, scandal, shame, loss and a name that worked like a diplomat's passport, providing access and immunity. She could not relate. The Martin name would not open any doors. Her father had emigrated from the Bahamas. Her mother was from Georgia. They were entry-level middle class at best. The family home was their one asset. When they died unexpectedly, she and Arielle had sold it to cover the cost of the funeral and other expenses and split the rest. Eve had inherited from her grandmother, as well. Grandma Martin had left her and Arielle exactly ten grand each. The old school Caribbean woman never trusted banks and squirreled away her savings in tin boxes. For sentimental reasons, Eve had kept her inheritance in the same blue Danish butter cookie box that she had received it. The cash had come in handy when her accounts were frozen. It was as if her wise grandmother had known that a woman always needed liquid assets. All in all, her family had left Eve and Arielle in good shape. The rest of it, though, the scandal and shame, they had brought on themselves.

"You and Cammie seem to get along," she said.

Rafael raked his fingers along his jawline. "It's work, though. I'm not a family guy, Eve. I've never had a traditional family, and I don't know how the gears work."

None of that changed the fact that he could be a dream boss. Would he be moody or temperamental at work because of his family drama? If that were the case, she wouldn't wilt. Eve had worked with some major jerks in the past. "If you have a bad day at work, don't worry about me. I can take it."

"I wouldn't take my crap out on you," he said. "That's not what this is about."

"What then?"

He leaned back, hesitated. The breeze tousled his hair and she was suddenly jealous of the breeze. "Opening a luxury guest ranch this close to the TCC makes good business sense," he said. "When this property came up for sale, I grabbed it. But Royal is Tobias's territory. Something about this doesn't sit right."

"Just to be clear—Tobias is your dad. Correct?"

"Don't call him that."

Oops! Eve reached for her coffee cup. "Noted."

"Sorry," he said, sheepish. "That came out harsh."

"Look," she said. "It's not my business, but the way I see it Royal is Arias territory, too."

A current of understanding passed between them. Eve got it now. This new endeavor was a monument to his mother disguised as a guest ranch for the discerning traveler. Rafael was putting down a marker. His goal was to raise the Arias name, flip Tobias the bird and remind all of Royal the son of scandal was back.

"I've been tossing money around like confetti on this project and…some other things. I need to be reined in. That's where your job would come in."

God bless the person who had to rein in Rafael Arias Wentworth. She bet wild horses were more readily tamed.

"Do I even have a job?" she asked testily. This interview had gone off the rails. There was no point beating around the bush anymore.

"The job is yours, Eve," he said. "Just take it already. Or are you going to demand a fitness test?"

The job is yours. Eve let out a long breath. She had a job. Praise God! Now it was time to get serious. She dropped her elbows on the table and interlaced her fingers. "In that case, let's talk money."

Rafael's eyes flashed. You'd have thought she'd asked him to talk dirty to her. Was money his love language? What a coincidence! It was hers, too.

"Alright," he said. "Let's talk. Give me your number."

"I'm not cheap."

"Shock me."

"Forty thousand."

"Come on, Eve. Is that a joke?"

"I've done the research," she said, offended. "Thirty-five thousand is the average salary of an executive assistant in Royal."

"You'll have more than administrative duties. I want you in charge of the budget."

Her heart fluttered. Was that what he meant by reining him in? Getting a hold on the budget? He was likely going overboard with the renovation. He could build this place into the Taj Majal and it wouldn't change anything. Her advice was to leave "family vendetta" off the budget.

"Is that something you'd be interested in?" he asked.

"Very much."

Spreadsheets, budgets and reports were her thing. She enjoyed making sense of numbers. It was assuredly the most boring skill set known to man, but Eve didn't care.

"Did I mention this job includes some travel? Are you comfortable with that?"

"I am, to some extent. I wouldn't want to be away from Micah for too long."

"I understand," he said. "An overnight trip now and then to visit a distributor or location site. Nothing more involved than that."

No adjoining suites. No dinners in bathrobes. No kissing on the floor. No falling asleep in his arms. "No problem."

"Knowing all of that, what's your number?"

"Forty-five thousand?"

"Oh, Eve." He balled up his cloth napkin and tossed it onto the table. "You can't tiptoe into negotiations."

The chef arrived with their omelets. Eve thanked him. It looked and smelled delicious. Too bad her stomach was in knots.

"Rafael," she said a moment later. "I don't have the winning hand here."

"Yes, you do," he said. "All signs point to you as the ideal candidate. I need someone competent who is willing to start right away. You're in a position to do that. More importantly, I need someone I can trust. So, from where I sit, your hand looks pretty good. Play it."

"I want sixty-five thousand to handle the administrative work, plus the budget and expense reports."

"Done."

Eve brightened. "Really?"

"The standard answer is, 'I can live with that.'"

She really could. This meant a decent life for her and Micah, whether they found his wayward father or not. In a gesture that was definitively not interview appropriate, she reached over and covered his hand with hers. "Thanks. You won't be sorry."

His expression clouded and something inside Eve collapsed. The elephant in the room, or gazebo in this case, had to be addressed. "Rafael," she said, her heart aching, "I want you, but I *need* this job."

His gaze did not flicker, even as the light in his eyes dimmed. "Am I the fantasy that you're setting aside to focus on reality?"

Eve did not reply. The answer was obvious.

Rafael withdrew his hand from beneath hers. "*Bienvenida al rancho*, Ms. Martin," he said. "Can you start on Monday?"

Eve didn't reply to that, either. The answer was obvious, too.

Ten

I want you, but I need this job.

Sitting across a table from Tobias Wentworth, Rafael stewed. Eve had said those words so matter-of-factly, almost without feeling. Well, he wanted her, too, but couldn't turn it off and on like she could. The slow fire they'd lit in the garden at the TCC had quickly grown wild and out of control. He thought about her every waking hour. He wanted to finish what they'd started at the Belleview. It wasn't the same for her; she could take it or leave it.

"Are those fries any good?" Tobias asked.

"Pretty good."

They were at their usual table at their usual meeting spot, the Colt Room at the Cattleman's Club. They'd met for dinner instead of lunch. Rafael had rescheduled on account of his late breakfast with Eve. Still, he ordered his usual burger and munched on the seasoned fries without tasting them.

"You're stabbing the damn things with your fork like you have something against them," Tobias said. "Looks personal."

Rafael stared at his silver-haired, blue-eyed "dad" who could always read his moods. Some things never changed.

Rafael had returned to Royal on the promise that Tobias was a changed man. He'd given up his money-hungry ways and started a charitable foundation to prove it. It had only taken the death of the woman he loved to bring that drastic change about. Much like it had taken the death of his mistress, Rafael's mother, for Tobias to acknowledge Rafael and bless him with the Wentworth name. Why did a good woman have to die just to nudge this man down the right path was the question Rafael wanted answered.

"It's been a tricky week," he mumbled.

Tobias cut into his steak. "I heard about the construction accident."

"Yeah, that was something," Rafael said. "But did you hear about the champagne tower that collapsed in the ballroom? That was a catastrophe."

"Oh, yeah," Tobias said with a chuckle. "I would have liked to see it."

For a cranky old man, Tobias could be good company.

"I heard from Cammie that you've taken on a mentee and doing a good job with it."

Tobias's nonprofit venture provided assistance and support to the children of first responders. Cammie had joined as the organization's director and was steering it well. Rafael's receptionist, Audrey, had received a scholarship and was putting it to good use. She worked mornings and attended evening classes at the local college. When Cammie brought up Lucas, a clever kid who was at risk of dropping out of high school, Rafael had offered to meet with him. Now he couldn't shake the kid off—not that he wanted to.

"You know how it is," Rafael said, brushing off the praise. "Give a kid some attention, and they end up clinging to you for life."

"No," Tobias said. "I don't know how it is."

Rafael felt a pang of something. It couldn't be guilt. Tobias's relationships with his kids were tenuous at best. At some point, there hadn't been any relationship to speak of, so really, this was progress. The man should be counting his blessings.

"Stick with me," Rafael said. "I'll teach you a few tricks."

As much as he loved his work, Rafael had never wished away a weekend. Yet he'd spent his Sunday just waiting for Monday to come around. He couldn't wait to see Eve. He knew that he had to stay away from her, treat her like any other employee, but he wasn't sure how he'd go about it. In the recesses of his imagination, he replayed the images of their night together. He was stuck on the moment when she had offered him her naked body. Eve didn't play at seduction. As with everything else, she'd been direct and matter-of-fact, and it was sexy as hell. With so much unfinished business between them, how could he pretend it wasn't killing him? How could he hide it?

Finally, it was Monday. Rafael left it to Dan to greet

Eve and show her the ropes as he pretended to go about business as usual. Eve was in good, capable hands. Dan was his second-in-command. Originally from Houston, he had jumped at the opportunity to relocate from Fort Lauderdale to Royal to help set up the guest ranch. Rafael had intended to stay out of the way for now and maybe stop by her office to welcome her later in the day. Yet Dan called almost straightaway to conference him into their meeting. "Our new hire has some…concerns on what she calls the Cadillac of benefit packages."

Dan was a Black, gay, army veteran who, as he put it, did not tolerate foolishness.

"Is that right?" Rafael said.

"Yes, sir. It is."

Her voice came through the speakerphone loud and clear, combative as ever. Rafael nearly burst with happiness. He reclined in his desk chair and joined his hands behind his head. "Alright. Let's hear it."

"We'll begin with the actual Cadillac," Dan said.

Rafael had picked out the vehicle himself. "Eve, you object to a company car?"

"Did my predecessor have a company car?" she asked.

Rafael tossed the question to Dan, her predecessor. "Did you, Dan?"

"I had a company truck," Dan replied flatly. "That's more my speed. Would you prefer a truck?"

"No, I wouldn't," Eve said. "But a Cadillac…"

"It's not an Escalade or anything," Dan said. "It's a compact SUV, solid, reliable and very stylish."

"Fine!" she said.

Rafael had to mute the phone to laugh. Meanwhile,

Dan moved on to the next topic. "We covered health insurance. No objections there."

"None," Eve said. "And thank you."

"Now to accommodations," Dan said. "Here are the keys to the residence. Suite 3A is on the top floor. The views are partially obscured, but I think you'll like it."

"A suite? Really?"

"We don't have anything smaller, Eve," Rafael said. "And the view is fine."

"Did my predecessor have a suite in the residence?"

"Didn't need one," Dan said. "My fiancé and I are renting a bungalow in town."

"I don't need one, either," Eve protested. "I live in town, too."

"You sure about that?" Dan quipped.

"Mr. Arias, I would like to speak to you in person."

Rafael could think of nothing he'd like more. "I have an open door policy, Ms. Martin. Come on by."

She stormed into his office moments later, looking pretty and fresh in a lemon drop yellow dress. Her expression was tart.

"It's too much!" she exclaimed.

"Good morning, Eve. Have a seat."

She ignored him. "Seriously, what are you doing? A car? A suite?"

"The package is tailored to your needs. In your case, you need a car and a shorter commute."

"A company car is a Nissan or Toyota, not a Cadillac."

"I like to buy American."

"You drive a Jaguar!"

"You know too much about me," he said with a laugh. She gave him a sharp look, cutting off his laughter at the source. "Why not let me help you?" he asked. "It makes no difference to me. At this point, it's all Monopoly money exchanging hands."

In his heyday, Tobias Wentworth had a reputation of being a hard-ass boss and a miserly one at that. Rafael was determined to run his businesses differently. That meant meeting his staff's needs and treating them like people from the start, not as a means of damage control when things went awry.

Eve came closer, her hands little tight fists at her sides. In a thin voice, she said, "I don't want to owe you anything."

"The suite is available. If you don't move in, it'll just sit there empty."

The intercom buzzed, and Audrey's voice crackled through the speaker. "Mary Richardson is on line 1."

Mary Richardson, along with her husband, Keith, owned the neighboring South Point Motel. Rafael had been waiting for this call. He asked Eve to give him a minute. She went over to the couch, but the call was over by the time she got settled. He'd been summoned by his neighbor.

"Don't get comfortable," he said. "We've got work to do."

Eleven

The South Point Motel had seen better days. Or was it that Eve was enchanted with the splendor of Casa Arias, just next door. Mary and Keith Richardson were plain-spoken individuals. They were not at all enchanted with their new neighbor or his plans for their property. But, as Mary Richardson said, they were at the end of the road. It was time for them to retire. Their adult children were not interested in managing a run-down motel. After a family meeting, they'd agreed to sell. "How to go about it is the question," Mary said.

"How do you want to go about it?" Rafael asked.

"We could put it on the market and see what bites, but why play that game?"

"There's no reason we can't come to an agreement."

Eve didn't need a briefing to understand the appeal of the Richardsons' property. The motel stood at the corner of a busy intersection. On the drive over, Rafael shared his plan to convert the building into a day spa, the type of business that would attract clients. But his real interest in the motel was its access to the main roads. As it was, Casa Arias was accessible only by a narrow side street. It wasn't ideal. Joining the two properties would greatly increase accessibility.

"Hold on." Keith spoke up for the first time. "The way I see it, you need us more than the other way around."

Rafael slid a glance Keith's way. "Funny. That's not how I see it at all."

Eve could not turn away from Rafael. She saw something in those dark eyes, gleaming like a razor's edge. It sent a shiver down her spine. Try as Rafael might to distance and distinguish himself from his family name, he was his father's son.

The meeting was inconclusive. Rafael was uncharacteristically silent on the drive back to his property. Eve would pay for his thoughts. He'd been wrong earlier. She did not know enough about him, and she was endlessly curious.

He pulled into his reserved spot. She reached for the door handle and he reached for her, curling a hand around her wrist. His touch was light, but the ribbon of heat coiled up her arm and held tight. He hadn't touched her since, well, that night when he'd touched her all over. God help her; the memory of that night still held her captive.

"Sorry I pressured you about moving in," he said. "Just wanted to help. Didn't mean to make you uncomfortable."

He released her and stepped out of the car. She followed him into the main house and up to the second floor. He directed her to her office then walked away, leaving her feeling lost, disoriented and confused.

Eve was ready to leave for the day when Dan chased her down the hall. "Ms. Martin! Hold on! I have your keys. The car is serviced and ready."

He dropped the key fob in her hand. She stared at it, wondering whether her Airbnb host offered overnight parking.

"I'll show you to it," Dan said.

He took her to the employee lot. A sleek, red SUV caught her eye. She loved it. Later, she'd sit Rafael down for a talk on what counted as reasonable business acquisitions and expenditures. For now, though, she couldn't wait to climb behind the wheel. "It's a beauty."

"What did I tell you?" Dan boasted.

"Tell me the truth," Eve said. "He buys these cars just for the chance to drive them."

"It's a lease, but yeah."

"Help me set up the Bluetooth?"

"No problem."

Dan did more than set up the Bluetooth. He adjusted the seat to her height, added the local public radio station to her list of favorites and entered her home address into the navigation system. She thanked him and wished him good-night. Once settled behind the wheel, she punched in Cammie and Drake's address and drove straight over. It had been a long day. She needed to hold her nephew.

Two weeks into the job and Eve was feeling settled, and that was unsettling in and of itself. She learned the

ropes. She knew her way to the restroom, breakroom
and gym. She'd joined the morning coffee circle led
by Audrey. Her days were shaped into a routine. She
worked until five and, if she did not have a therapy appointment, she took off to spend time with Micah. For
the most part, Rafael's affairs were in order and it was
a while until she encountered her first red flag. Eve
was no expert, but a proposal from a local design firm
seemed to run a bit high. She used that excuse to sched-
ule an emergency meeting with her boss.

Rafael had been avoiding her or, as he put it, "giving her space." He assured her that he was only a phone
call away. She could read him pretty well. These new
roles they'd assigned to themselves were constricting.
By taking this job, she'd hijacked the ship and changed
the course of their relationship. They'd been on their
way to becoming something other than employer and
employee. When she heard his voice down the hall, regret tied a rope around her heart. When she ate lunch
alone at her desk, she wished they could, if only for a
moment, sit, talk and laugh like that first night. Honestly, she would be willing to dock one week's pay for
it. Finally, she had a legitimate excuse to seek him out.
When she called, he reminded her of his open door policy and told her to swing by whenever.

In her old workplace, where ninja warrior skills were
required to leap from one rung of a ladder to the next,
there was no swinging by anywhere to speak with the
top brass. She swung by and found that he was not
alone. A teenage boy in a pressed button-down shirt
sat in one of the two leather swivel guest chairs. Rafael was seated next to him, his feet propped up on his

desk. They were sipping milkshakes and watching a Michael Jordan documentary on the wall-mounted TV.

"What's going on here?" Eve demanded, true to her schoolmarm self.

Rafael swiveled lazily in her direction. Eve wanted to swivel in the opposite direction and run down the hall. The urge to go to him, kiss him, ball up on his lap and set her head on his chest had come on suddenly and in the most violent way. When Eve had asked for this job, it was with the understanding that she would pack away all the feelings he stirred up in her. She'd struck that deal with herself and had entered into it discreetly, advisedly and soberly. Nothing had changed. She couldn't afford to mess this up. Very soon, she'd finish PT, get her doctor to sign off to regain custody of Micah and would have to provide for him. She still very much needed this job.

"Ms. Martin," he said. "Come in. Meet Lucas, my…" To Lucas, he said, "What are you again?"

"You're my mentor," Lucas said. "I think the word you're looking for is *mentee*."

"I think the word I'm looking for is wise ass."

"That's two words." Lucas turned to Eve for confirmation. "Am I right?"

"Leave her out of this," Rafael scolded.

"He's new to this," Lucas said. "It's only been six weeks or so of mentoring. He's doing okay, but we'll see how it goes."

"This is Evelyn Martin, my new executive assistant."

Eve stepped forward. "Nice meeting you, Lucas."

The boy grinned and gave her a double thumbs-up with greasy thumbs, a crumpled hamburger wrapper clutched in one hand. Lucas would grow up to be a handsome man someday. For now, though, he was all curly dark hair, mischievous grins, brown sunbaked skin and long, wiry limbs.

Rafael's eyes were on her, as gentle as his tone. "What do you have for me?"

Eve blinked, her brain blank. "I...uh...flagged something on the design firm's proposal."

"Tell me," he said.

"They've proposed marble for the spa."

"Is that bad?" he asked.

Lucas slurped his milkshake. "Gotta have that marble bling!"

"Marble is expensive," Eve explained. "Plus, it's impractical. It's great for some areas but not the best choice for the spa treatment rooms."

"What do you suggest?" Rafael asked.

"Quartz. Far more resistant, equally beautiful."

He seemed doubtful. "Is it, though?"

"I thought you might have doubts so I went out and got samples." During her lunch break, she'd gone to the nearest big box home improvement store. Eve opened the small cardboard box she'd brought with her and produced marble and quartz square tiles. Holding them up like a TV infomercial host, she said, "See for yourself."

Rafael and Lucas roared. For a split second she thought her masterful presentation had earned her a standing ovation, but nothing could be further than the truth. Rafael and Lucas were focused on the television screen, where Michael Jordan had leaped across the court and dunked a ball into the basket.

Lucas punched the air. "The man can fly!"

Rafael fell back in his seat, undone. "It gets me every time. Every damn time."

The two switched to Spanish, praising the prowess of the legendary basketball star. Eve, incensed, held up the samples. "Excuse me!"

Rafael snapped to attention, contrite. "I'm sorry, Ms. Martin. You were saying."

The formal "Ms. Martin" grated on her nerves. "You're his mentor. Shouldn't you be teaching him something?"

Rafael snapped the remote control off his desk and hit pause. Lucas groaned in protest, but Rafael silenced him. "She's right," he said. "The first thing I'm going to teach you is to respect your employees' time. Go on, Ms. Martin."

Eve felt foolish. After all, she'd barged in and dampened their fun. "You could save up to fifty dollars a square foot. Not to mention the expense of upkeep."

Rafael patted his pockets and found his phone. He dialed a number. "Yeah, Jason, I'd like a revised budget proposal to swap out marble for quartz in the spa treatment rooms. Comb through for any other cost saving options, and we'll see you Wednesday…Sounds good." He ended the call. "Damn! I feel productive."

Lucas rested a hand on his shoulder. "Good job, *jefe*."

Eve folded her arms across her chest. These two were clowns! She couldn't help but think back at her own high school internships, mainly how dull they'd been. She was assigned thankless tasks, making copies and fetching coffee, for the privilege of adding a company's name to her résumé. She hadn't learned a damn thing except how to make herself small and stay out of the way. She did not know anything about Lucas, but she would bet his parents were not TCC members. Rafael was teaching him a lesson: you could be successful and accessible. There was no need for a gilded cage. Eve was learning something, too. It was okay to have a little fun at work.

She reached for the remote and pressed play. "It's the goofy Mr. Clean earring that bugs me."

Lucas came back to life. "It's the source of his power!"

Rafael stood, took the samples from her clutched hands and eased her into the seat he'd just vacated. "Chocolate or vanilla?"

He was offering her a milkshake. "Strawberry?"

The corner of his mouth curved into a teasing smile. "You got it."

That evening, Eve went to spend time with Micah. After a solid half hour of tummy time, she sat on the floor, scooped her nephew up and settled him on her lap. She rocked and hummed a sad little lullaby her Bahamian grandmother used to sing to her and Arielle. *Hush little baby...my trials soon be over...* She could not sing that song without thinking of the fate of her sister, whom she prayed was at peace. But Eve's trials were over, too.

She'd been through the worst of it and, finally, things were looking up. For the longest time, Eve had adopted a defensive posture, just trying to protect herself and Micah. Now was the time to go on the offense, gain ground and make up for all she'd lost. She claimed to want a better future, for her nephew and herself. It had been her singular focus all those weeks spent in the hospital, alone, depressed and scared. But she could see now that her priorities were as scattered as the colorful blocks flung about the nursery.

Eve made some decisions. She'd move into the suite at the residence. Dan had given her a tour just to further entice her. It was the exact layout of her tiny efficiency except triple the size, airy and bright. It had gleaming wood floors, a modern kitchen, and, naturally, polished marble surfaces. A large bay window faced west. As far as she could tell, the only obstruction was the fine tops of pine trees. Eve was sure the sunsets would be miraculous.

By moving into the residence, she would eliminate the taxing commute. The money saved on rent would go to paying off her debts. Win-win-win.

Eve had been wrong about Rafael. Men like him were good for more than one thing. He was a business-man, cunning when it suited him. Good at seizing op-portunities. Good at making money. Those were the skills that she had to develop. Since he was so intent on helping her, maybe he could help her draft a busi-ness plan of her own.

Micah fell asleep in her arms. As his breathing steadied, Eve slipped out her phone and dialed Rafael's number for the first time. He answered straightaway, his voice betraying his disbelief. "Eve? Is everything okay?"

"I'm moving into the residence."

"You are?"

"Yes," she said. "How soon can I move in?"

"Now… I'll help you pack."

"No," she said. "I can manage."

She'd turned him down mostly out of habit, but she really didn't have very much to pack.

"You're sure you don't need help to pack the car? Then haul it all up to the third floor of the residence?"

He had a point. With her heart condition, she shouldn't be lifting anything heavy. Her doctor would not approve. "Okay! Fine! Come by tonight."

"Send me your address."

Twelve

Rafael ducked out of a dinner party hosted by a state representative to drive across town and help Eve pack. He couldn't wait to see her again. By his own clever calculation, he'd ensured that he would see her every day from this day on. His generous offer had a selfish motive, designed to keep her close. It wasn't the thing a good and charitable person would do, which made him want to call her and say "See? You were wrong about me. I'm not the Good Samaritan of your dreams." But that would freak her out and rightly so.

He pulled up to her address. Eve lived in a converted-garage-turned-Airbnb. It was as dreary as he'd imagined. Selfish motives or no, he could not allow her to stay here.

She opened the door, wearing heather-gray leggings and a small, tight, yellow T-shirt with a smiley face stretched across her breasts. The bright color played up her brown skin nicely. She took a step back. "Had I known this was a fancy packing event, I would have thrown on my one cocktail dress."

"The red one?" he asked, suddenly excited.

"No," she said. "The other one."

"That makes two."

"Who's counting?"

"I am," he said. "Just for accuracy. May I come in?"

She looked at him appraisingly. "I don't think so."

"I had a thing," he said, explaining away his dark suit. "I'll lose the jacket and roll up my sleeves."

"Please! I love when you do that."

Rafael played back the reel of every single one of their encounters until he found it: that night in the garden. She sat on the stone bench, moonlight adding sparkle to her soulful eyes. He'd draped his jacket over her shoulders, loosened his tie and rolled up his sleeves. He knew they were on the verge of something that night, some grand adventure, and had refused to let the night end.

"Come in," she said.

He stepped inside and shut the door behind him.

The kitchen, the bedroom, the tiny seating area were all crammed in one space. Rafael wasn't a snob. He'd lived in smaller places when he left home at seventeen. But at seventeen, he didn't care where he lived.

She pointed to the wine and water glasses lined up on the kitchen countertop. "If you could wrap those in newspaper, that would be great."

Eve folded laundry at the foot of her bed. He got to work, but she made a point not to look at him when he slipped off the jacket.

"Would you like something to drink?" she asked.

"Sure. Thanks."

She left the basket of laundry and went to the refrigerator, pulled out a bottle of fruit-flavored sparkling water and filled two glasses that he had not yet wrapped. "The first thing I did when I moved in was to buy stemware at the big box store to enjoy a cool beverage like a lady."

"I approve," he said. "Sounds like you've got your priorities in order."

"Speaking of priorities, I've been thinking," she said. "How did you get into the hospitality industry?"

"My friends used to call my crappy little apartment in Miami Beach a hostel," he said. "It was the one place they could crash, take a nap or a shower. The refrigerator was always stocked. After college, I applied for a job at a hotel and was hired on the spot. The owner was...kind. He took the time to show me the business. When he got sick and was ready to sell, he arranged for me to get a loan." Rafael took a sip of sparkling water and grimaced. "He became a father figure to me, you know? What he did allowed me to come back to Royal a success. Before you ask, the answer is no. I didn't take a dime of my father's money."

Rafael's hands were trembling. He pressed them onto the butcher-block countertop to steady them. Funny how her simple question had drawn so much out of him.

"How are things with your father now?" she asked.

He grabbed a delicate wineglass and wrapped it in the Sunday sports page. "We meet for lunch once a week or so. That's the long and short of it. We're never going to be the perfect father and son. We're not playing catch in his mansion's backyard."

"No one plays catch with their kids," she said with a little laugh. "That's what Little League is for."

"Are you close with your parents?" he asked.

"While they were alive. Sure."

God! What this woman had been through... "Sorry, Eve."

She brushed the condolence away. "My mother and I never did the typical mother-daughter things. She didn't teach me how to sew or wear makeup. She didn't even teach me much about bras. I had to sort all that out myself. But she loved me unconditionally. See my point?"

"Your mother was a lovely person. My father is Tobias."

"Well, that's true."

Her expression went soft. He turned away, taking a sip with a painful expression. She wasn't the only one who couldn't stomach pity. When their eyes met again, she was still studying him.

"You hate it, don't you?" she said.

"This sparkling stuff?" He set down the glass. "So much. Do you have anything else? Beer?"

"Sorry, I don't," she said. "They sell beer at the corner store."

He grabbed his car keys off the counter. "Great. Let's go!"

"Put away your keys. It's a short walk and parking is a hassle." She emptied their glasses into the sink. "Let's order pizza, too. Up for it?"

He was up for anything, apart from discussing the past. It was done, and there was nothing to be gained by digging up those old bones.

After calling the pizzeria, she and Rafael took off into the night. They argued about toppings on their way

to the store and crusts on their way back. She paused to
tie her laces just as Rafael brought up *tlayuda*, a Mexican tortilla. Having never tried it, Eve had no opinion
on the dish. That didn't stop Rafael from launching into
an impassioned defense of the street food favorite. Right
then, a sprinkler embedded in the hedge that lined the
sidewalk burst into action. A hard stream of cold water
slapped her in the face. Eve cried out with outrage. The
jet reversed course and struck her in the back of the
head. She heard Rafael swear through the ringing in
her ears. She was vaguely aware that he dropped the
convenience store bag of snacks and grabbed her, pulling her out of the jet's path.

"Why am I always wet when I'm around you?" She
caught the double entendre and tried, very clumsily, to
walk the comment back. "God! I didn't mean for it to
sound like that."

"Sound like what?" Rafael said distractedly. For
some reason, he was undressing right on the sidewalk.

"What are you doing?"

He was very obviously unbuttoning his shirt. The
slow reveal of his smooth and sculpted chest had made
up for the indignity of getting sprayed in the face.

"Covering you up. You're going to freeze."

He draped his dress shirt over her shoulders. His
voice warmed her more than the thin extra layer, yet
she reveled in it. Rafael raised her chin with the tip of
his finger and inspected her face. With the back of his
hand, he blotted her cheeks dry. The gesture was unexpectedly tender. The way he looked after her, those sudden displays of tenderness, got to her. Or maybe it was
his bare, sculpted chest and the way his golden brown

skin shimmered in the lamplight. Either way, he got to her—there was no denying it.

"Is this about your grandmother again?" she asked for the sake of making chitchat. "Because she's wrong. I won't catch pneumonia. I'll be fine."

"Take that back," he said. "Abuela Carla was never wrong."

She caught his use of the past tense. "I had an opinionated grandmother, too, you know," she said. "She would have fixed me a cup of ginger tea and told me to go to bed."

"Sounds like our grandmothers would have gotten along." He rubbed her arms, still trying to generate heat. It was wholly unnecessary. His shirt had wrapped her in his scent, and it warmed her to the core.

"If our grandmothers are looking down at us right now, they're probably wondering what we're squabbling about."

"Doubt it," he said, and scooped up the bag that he'd dropped to come to her aid. The muscles of his back rippled as he moved. "They're probably wondering why we aren't getting busy making babies."

"For the last time!" Eve cried, feeling defensive. "No one is trying to have your baby! Get that out of your head."

"Good! I don't even want kids."

The finality of his tone struck her. "Why not?"

"Not wired for it. That's all."

Eve vaguely remembered him saying as much during the unorthodox job interview. She hadn't realized he'd made it a lifestyle. That said, she wasn't about to lecture him about the joys of procreation. She wasn't sure she wanted kids herself. That choice, however, was no longer hers to make now that Micah had been left in her care.

"My family can't seem to get it right," Rafael said. "Let the generational curse die with me."

"If you're cursed," Eve said, "I don't want to be blessed."

"Ha!" He gestured for them to keep moving. They were only steps away from her door. She trotted after him. Although she hated to admit it, the night air had a bite to it and Eve was starting to feel chilly. At her door, he took her key from her. "I got it."

Once inside, she stepped out of her sneakers and arranged them neatly by the door. She was only buying time to gather herself. Maybe it was the sight of this half-dressed man entering her place, taking their purchases into the tiny kitchen, looking around for her when she failed to follow him any farther than the foyer, but she was coming undone. All her reasons for holding back, good reasons, solid reasons, sound reasons, crumbled.

"I'll get you a towel. Where do you keep them?"

Never mind a towel. Never mind his shirt, for that matter. She stripped it off and draped it on the back of one of her two dining chairs. Then she stripped off her T-shirt, which was properly drenched and could very well give her pneumonia. It slipped from her hands and fell to her feet. Rafael went still. She had seen that look in his eyes the night she kissed him in the lobby of the Belleview Inn.

"Do you think?" She took a step toward him at the cost of losing her nerve. Her voice came out strained. "Could we…just one time…maybe?"

Silence swirled around them. Rafael studied her, unhurried. Her hopes shattered with each passing second. She was about to tell him to forget it when he answered, his voice hoarse. "We can definitely just one time… maybe."

Eve rushed to him, wrapped her arms around his neck and pressed her sopping wet body to his. She must have knocked him off balance because they stumbled over together, landing on the carpeted floor. He brushed back her hair, took her face in his hands and held it as if she were a thing of rare beauty. A stone dislodged in her chest and the truth spilled out. "These last weeks have been terrible."

"Thank God!" He repeated the words under his breath in Spanish. *"Gracias a Dios!"*

"Rafael!" she scolded him.

His hands freely roamed her body. "I'm in hell, and I don't care who knows it."

She traced a finger down the length of his nose. "I'm in heaven now."

Rafael pinned her hands over her head and kissed her softly. Just as she eased into it, he withdrew and kissed her hard. Eve kissed back, hungrily, drunkenly, forgetting the complicated world just outside the door. In here, he was all hers. But then, as luck would have it, a brisk knock on her door brought everything to a screeching halt. A young voice cried, "Pizza!"

Eve groaned and Rafael buried his face in the curve of her neck. "Damn it!" he lamented.

No matter how they felt about it, the pizza delivery guy had done his job, and he wasn't going to leave until he got paid.

"Maybe he has condoms," she joked.

Rafael made a face. "*I* have condoms."

"Hey," Eve said. "You stocked up."

"After last time, I'm not taking chances."

Another knock on the door.

He pushed away, rising into a push-up. She missed the weight and heat of this body. "I'll take care of it."

She smashed his face between her hands. "You've got five minutes. Got that? And don't forget to tip."

He hopped to his feet. "Yes, ma'am!"

In the bathroom, Eve peeled off her soaking wet sports bra and dropped it into the sink. She caught her reflection in the mirror. Naked from the waist up, she looked wild. Eyes bright, lips swollen, cheeks taking on a raspberry flush. Most shocking was her hair. It had come loose from her ponytail. Eve's mother might not have taught her much about makeup, but she had obsessed over Eve's and Arielle's hair, always insisting they keep it neat and straight, never wild, never kinky, never a strand out of place.

She reached for a brush. For some reason, it was heavy as stone. She couldn't do it. She couldn't smooth out the lines and tuck the loose ends in place. What had she gained from following every damn rule in the book? Eve heard the front door slam shut. She put away the brush just as Rafael crowded the bathroom doorway. Their eyes met in the mirror.

"Knock, knock," he said.

She swiveled around to face him. "Just so we're clear. We're about to make a big mistake, aren't we?"

Rafael did not hesitate. "Oh, yeah. We're clear on that."

Eve loved the way he flew straight into the fire. "How about we make a deal?"

"Another deal?" he said. "Should I get my lawyer on the phone?"

Eve fell back against the vanity and gripped the edge of the countertop. "It's simple, really. You make me laugh and I'll make you—"

"Make me what?" he asked.

The answer she gave wasn't what she had cued up. "I'll make you feel a little less lonely in this town."

Rafael didn't say anything, but Eve knew she was right. Rafael Arias Wentworth was a charming, handsome, sexy, lonely man. He covered it with layers of charisma, but she saw through it. Like recognized like.

"Did you think this through?" he asked. "Sounds like a lopsided deal. I stand to receive far more than I'm asked to give."

"That's because you don't know the good it does me to laugh."

He rested his head on the doorframe and looked at her awhile. "Lucky for you, I love your laugh."

For all the heated glances they'd exchanged, it seemed to Eve they were seeing each other, bare and unvarnished, for the first time. He reached for the switch and killed the harsh overhead light and stood motionless in the soft light pouring in from the main room. Rafael in moonlight, in streetlight, in the pale light of a table lamp... He was unfailingly beautiful. Eve reached out to him. "Come here."

He kicked the door shut, came to her and hoisted her onto the vanity countertop. She worked on the buttons of the shirt he'd thrown on for the benefit of the pizza guy. Eve wanted to see him, touch him, explore his body. "You had your way last time," she said. "It's my turn."

"Well, now," he said in the dark. "Lucky me…"

Eve could swim in the currents of his voice. She swept her lips down the ridges of his throat. Her fingers found the hard knot of a nipple. She dipped her head and grazed it with her teeth. It was all it took to snap the thread that bound his self-control. Rafael cupped her breasts and returned the favor, his tongue circling her tender nipples before tugging them taut with his teeth. Eve arched forward, surrendering again. He slid his hands beneath the waist of her leggings and tugged them down her hips and, stepping back, down her legs. "So, you're always wet around me? I didn't know."

Eve burned with embarrassment. "Didn't think you caught that."

"Are you kidding?" With her leggings balled up on the tile floor, Rafael worked her underwear down her thighs.

"It was a joke."

"A joke?" He parted her knees and made room for himself. Her breath hitched as he dragged the back of a hand from a knee up. "I don't believe it."

With the pad of his thumb he proved her to be a liar. Eve leaned forward to kiss his parted lips then tilted backward until her hot skin met the cool mirror. Rafael buried his head between her thighs. She shivered at the feel of his tongue. He spread her wider, explored her deeper. Eve bit her lip and gripped his hair, but there was nothing she could do to slow the rush of pleasure that came embarrassingly fast. Rafael pushed away and gathered her in his arms, holding her, stroking her until she calmed down.

She whimpered and clung to him. "It's been a while."

"*That* I believe."

"Shut up!" Eve fumbled with the buckle of his belt, eager and impatient for more.

"Settle down, sweet," he teased.

He finished undressing, found the condom in his wallet and, with adept fingers, put it on. Eve was unsettled by the sight of him and undone when he took her hand and curled her fingers around him. "Put me inside you."

"Oh, my God…"

He kissed her forehead to reassure her, but made his demand clear. "Work with me."

Eve snapped out of her inertia and guided him inside her. Rafael braced himself with a hand on the mirror behind her and eased into her, slow and controlled. "Do you know what I think?" he asked.

She shook her head, her hair wild around her face. She didn't know anything except how good he felt inside her. "I think you need more than a good laugh."

Heaven help her. That was the truth.

Thirteen

The coast was clear. Audrey was not at her desk. Eve waited a moment then dashed, as fast as she could, across the reception hall. She'd almost made it to the elevators when she heard the young woman call out her name. "Eve! Come back here!"

Every morning, she and Audrey started their day with coffee and a little harmless workplace gossip. Audrey had a specific set of skills. She'd predicted Dan would be promoted weeks before it was announced. When Rafael expressed interest in the Richardsons' property, she was not in the least bit surprised. Generally, Eve enjoyed their chats. This morning, though, she worried Audrey would use those skills to see right into her guilt-ridden heart. There was no office gossip so juicy than the new executive assistant sleeping with the boss.

She and Rafael had agreed to one time, but the likelihood of them sticking to that agreement was slim. Eve had only left him a short while ago. They'd finished packing her things and drove to the residence in the small hours of the morning. After piling the few boxes and bags in her living room, he invited her to tour his suite, conveniently located down the hall. And then they tumbled into bed. Eve was certain that anyone with a little sense would pick up on it, let alone someone as perceptive as Audrey. It turned out to be a needless worry. Audrey was preoccupied with other things.

"You're coming tonight, right?"

"Where to?"

"The Cattleman's Club."

"Nope!" Eve's attitude toward the country club was simple: been there, done that. She had no desire to return and had the perfect excuse. "I'm not a member."

"You think I am?" Audrey said. "Tonight is the Valentine's Day fundraiser."

"Is today Valentine's Day?" Eve asked, alarmed. Had she really committed the cardinal sin of sleeping with someone new just before February 14? She would have to let Rafael know that he was under no obligation to buy her flowers.

"No, that's tomorrow. Tonight's the fundraiser. Everybody is going."

Eve walked backward toward the elevators. "Not me!"

"Come on, Eve! You have to go!"

"Not invited! This is the first I'm hearing of this."

"Everyone is invited," Audrey insisted. "We have a table for ten and ours is going to be the most fun." Before Eve could stop her, Audrey had Rafael on speaker-phone. "Good morning, Mr. Arias Wentworth."

"Morning, Audrey."

Rafael's voice cracked through the speaker. As distant as it was, it brought him back to her. She could feel his hard body and smell his hair.

"Just wanted to clear something up with you. Eve, here, seems to think she's not invited to tonight's fundraiser."

After a moment's hesitation, Rafael said, "Is that tonight?"

Audrey looked as if she might faint. "You didn't forget, did you?"

"Oh, no! God no!" Rafael replied hastily. "Could you please ask Eve to come see me?"

"Absolutely!" Audrey ended the call with a triumphant look on her pretty face. "The boss wants to see you."

The door to Rafael's office was wide open. Eve knocked anyway. He looked up and tossed a file aside. "Ms. Martin."

"Mr. Arias Wentworth, Audrey said you wanted to see me?"

His mouth twitched with a smile. "Very much. Come in."

She took a seat at one of the chairs facing his desk. Sometime last night, she'd stood naked in this man's kitchen eating ice cream from the carton. He'd licked chocolate syrup off her fingertips and called her his "Candy Apple Eve." She'd laughed and planted a sticky chocolate kiss into the palm of his hand. The memory flickered before her eyes. Hard as she tried, she could not blink it away.

"I'll be honest," he said. "I forgot all about this damn fundraiser."

She would be honest, too. "Good. I have zero interest."

Rafael rose from behind his desk in one smooth movement and came to stand before her. He was never more handsome than when freshly shaved, hair damp, and wearing a crisp shirt. Even so, she preferred him as she'd left him an hour earlier: hair disheveled, cheeks rough with stubble, waving goodbye to her from bed as she tiptoed out the door.

"Here's the thing," he said. "We're duty bound to attend."

"I think you're wrong."

"Cammie will be expecting us."

He said *we* and *us* so liberally. It flooded her heart with irrational joy. Still, she held firm. "Surely Cammie isn't expecting *me*."

"I reserved a table a while ago and you're on my staff," he said. "She'll wonder why I excluded you. Think of the optics."

"I'd rather not."

"If you won't do it for Cammie, and the good children she's raising money for, do it for me. Just think of how lonely I'm going to feel at that country club surrounded by all those people. You did promise to help me feel less lonely, or don't you remember?"

"I remember." She glared at him. "You're never going to let me live that down, are you?"

"Never."

"I'm just done with that place," Eve said. "Don't you remember what happened the last time I was there?"

"You met me."

Eve let out a dramatic sigh. There was no way she was ever going to let him down. "I guess it's back to the country club."

"Welcome to Royal," he said. "All roads lead to the TCC."

He pulled his phone from the pocket of his charcoal-gray trousers. "You're going to need a dress."

"Can't I wear whatever?"

"No, you can't."

"Is this a fundraiser or the Met Gala?"

"Eve, sweet, I don't make the rules," he said as he absently scrolled his phone.

Next thing he had her speak with a personal shopper. Eve gave the professional her size and style preferences and was assured a few options would be delivered to her door by 5:00 p.m. Then she handed him the phone. "Thanks, but let this be the last time. Okay? This can't be a thing."

"What do you mean?"

"You taking charge, taking care of things."

"You mean taking care of *you*, don't you?"

"Yep." That was exactly what she meant.

"This doesn't count," he said. "The fundraiser is for a worthy cause. I'm doing this for the kids."

"Give me a break! You'd forgotten all about the kids."

"I forgot about the fancy dinner, not the kids. Never the kids."

"Good to know your heart is in the right place."

"Always," he said. "Now there's one more thing. As

impatient as I am to stuff my face with shrimp cocktail tonight—"

"Don't be mean," she scolded him. "I'm sure they'll
come up with something more imaginative than shrimp
cocktail."

"You give them too much credit," he said. "But here's
the thing. I need to make a quick detour before we head
out to the club tonight."

Again with the *we*… "Are *we* going together?"

"That's a given," he said. "I'd be lonely without you."

Eve shot to her feet. "You're on a roll this morning!"

"That's because I had a great night!"

He was adorable. Eve felt the pull, tugging her toward him. This was dangerous territory. "About that,"
she said. "Tonight's event has a Valentine's Day theme."

He sat on the corner of his desk. "I'm aware."

"You're under no obligation to, you know, go all out
and treat me like…" She grappled for the right word
and drew a blank.

"My valentine?" he suggested.

"Yes."

"My candy apple?"

Eve's face caught fire. "Stop that."

"My caramel candy sweet?"

She had to get out of there. "I've got work to do."

He grinned at her. "Don't let me keep you."

The trouble was, she thought, on her way to her office, she so very much wanted him to keep her…and
never let her go.

Fourteen

That evening, Rafael pulled up to Manny Suarez's auto shop. Eve looked out the passenger seat window, taking in the nondescript facade. "So, is this where you were the night we met?"

The night we met… He liked how that sounded. "You guessed it."

"And what is this place?"

"You'll see."

He got out of the car and came around to assist her. It was more than the gentlemanly thing to do. The seats of the sports car were low. Eve claimed to be progressing with physical therapy, yet she might still need assistance.

"Is this your pre-TCC ritual then? A drive to the wild side?"

He escorted her to the shop's door. "No, it just worked out like that."

He was here to finalize his selection of leather for the Camaro's seats. Manny flung the door open. "Bro! You brought a lady friend."

Rafael ignored the quip and introduced Eve to Manny.

"Good to meet you," Manny said. "Are you two heading off to the fancy Valentine's dance?"

"As a matter of fact we are," Rafael said.

"This is not a date," Eve said. "We're not dating."

Manny clapped. "Shot down!"

When Rafael swiveled to confront her, he lost his breath. Against the drab concrete gray walls of the shop, she was vibrant in a slinky red dress. This morning she'd told his personal shopper that she preferred color to black, and red was her favorite color of all. He'd made a mental note and filed it under miscellaneous things he knew about Eve. Tomorrow he'd order red roses.

She caught his eyes and spoke deliberately slow to ensure he caught her meaning. "We're attending the fundraiser in our professional capacity."

"Right," he said.

Manny tore open a bag of tortilla chips. "My wife made fresh guac. Want some?"

"Absolutely."

Manny entertained Eve with stories about his pet dogs. Something swelled inside Rafael. Her laughter was his, hard-won and prized. He wished he could hold her hand or touch her or display any form of affection without his gesture being met with a hard stare.

Back in the showroom, Manny tossed him a booklet. "Here are the swatches I wanted you to see. I have to put in the order by tomorrow so the suppliers in Italy can get it to me on time."

Rafael flipped through the booklet of leather swatches, ranging in color from cognac to deep bark brown. Eve approached and rested a hand on his wrist. "Those are gorgeous."

"Think so?" he said. "Pick one."

She tapped on a square of caramel-hued leather. His sweet, caramel candy apple Eve... "Good choice." He showed the swatch to Manny. "We'll go with this."

"What's it for?" she asked.

"You don't know?" Manny wiped his hands on a paper napkin. "You're in for a treat."

Eve looked to him for confirmation. "Really?"

Rafael was suddenly nervous. What would she think? He was burning steep stacks of cash on this project. That money could have easily changed her life or done a lot of good for someone. "We don't have time," Rafael said.

"But we drove all this way!"

"You got fresh guac out of it."

"That was good guac," she conceded. Nonetheless, she followed Manny to the back of the shop. He unveiled Rafael's car with his usual flourish. Rafael hadn't seen it in a few days. The strong, muscular build of the vehicle was all the more evident now that the old paint had been scraped off.

"You're...repairing an old car?"

"Restoring." Manny corrected her, defending his trade. "We're restoring a vintage '69 Camaro." He pulled up a photo on his phone and showed it to Eve. "This is what it'll look like when I'm done."

Eve studied the photo. "Hold up! You're going to make *this* look like *that*."

"That's what I do," Manny said.

"Like how? By magic?"

"No magic! Skill!"

She sought out Rafael. He braced himself for the blow of her disapproval. Instead, she looked amused. "There's no reining you in, is there?"

He grinned, relieved. "Afraid not!"

"I'm afraid to ask how much this will cost," Eve said.

"Don't be scared," Manny said. "I'll tell you. Homeboy is about to drop—"

"Look at the time! Eve, let's get going." She shot him a look and he shrugged. "TCC rule number 110: Don't be late for dinner."

"I'm pretty sure that's rule number one."

"No," he said. "That would be pay your dues."

"Naturally."

Manny escorted them to the door. "Bye, kids! Have fun at the dance! Make good choices!"

They arrived late anyway. The cocktail hour was over, and the guests were seated for dinner. Tables were set up in the grand ballroom. Every table had a blooming red centerpiece in keeping with the night's theme, but wisely, no one had erected a champagne tower. Rafael paused at the entrance to tug at the cuffs of his shirt and adjust the links, readying himself for battle. In the past, his instinct and concern had always been to protect himself. Tonight, he had the added responsibility of protecting Eve. He'd led her to the lion's den. He would not allow anyone to tear her apart.

"Ready?" he asked.

She nodded. "Uh-huh."

He saw the fear in her eyes. "Just remember the golden rule—small talk only. Keep the chitchat brief and brisk."

"Got it."

"You look sweet enough to suck on in that dress."

She startled, eyes dancing. "Way to keep it brief and brisk, Mr. Arias Wentworth."

"I want you to know that's all I'll be thinking about all night. Got that?"

"Got it."

"Don't worry about them." He nodded toward the packed dining room. "Worry about me."

She very discreetly stroked his arm. "I'm a multi-tasker. I can do both."

Rafael pushed out a laugh. As it turned out, he could multitask, too. He checked out the dining room and clocked Tobias at the head table along with Cammie and Drake. In his classic black tuxedo, Tobias looked good but he was not the formidable man who had terrorized his youth. And yet Rafael felt pressure build inside him. It never failed. One look from his father could undo all his plans, leave him doubting his worth. Each time they met, Rafael had to mentally reset the clock. He was not a lost teenager. He was independent, successful, no longer cowering under his father's shadow or struggling to get out from under his thumb.

Eve stepped closer to him and placed a hand on his shoulder. "Are you ready?" she asked.

He glanced at her and fell headfirst into the depths of her brown eyes. A ribbon of heat wrapped around his heart. *I'll make you feel a little less lonely in this town.* He had not taken that promise seriously. After all, how could she? Feeling alone, apart, unwelcomed was part and parcel of his identity. He would not relinquish it. It had made him the man he was today. But Eve's hand on his shoulder made him want to reconsider.

"You two make an *adorable* couple!" a woman exclaimed. Before Rafael could do anything about it, P&J
had accosted them.

"Is this date night?" Jennifer Carlton asked.

"No," Rafael said flatly. "This is a work event."

Jennifer winked. "I gotcha."

Paul Carlton voiced other concerns. "Have you heard
from the Richardsons? My sources say they're ready
to make a move. Now if you need a broker, I'm standing at the ready."

"I appreciate it," Rafael said.

"We're late as usual," Jennifer said. "Enjoy your
night, you two!"

Rafael waved them off, but Eve stood petrified. He
reached for her hand. "What's the matter?"

"They think we're a couple," she said. "And it's my
fault. If I hadn't kissed you at the Belleview Inn—"

"I wouldn't trade that kiss for anything in the world."

"Yeah, but now you're linked to another Martin sister."

He really didn't like where she was headed with this.
"I never met your sister," he said. "You, however, could
put up a chain-link fence around me and I wouldn't
mind."

They'd loaded so much baggage onto their leaky
boat, they were sure to go under. Not tonight, though.
He was going to paddle like hell to get them to shore.

Eve's eyes went misty, betraying her emotion, but her
lips twisted in a smile when she said, "The poet laure-
ate of Royal, Texas, has nothing on you."

"I've got skills," he said. "If you're ready, we should
first pay our respects to King Tobias."

She nodded. "Let's do this."

* * *

Tobias rose to greet them. He clasped Rafael's hand in his and said, a little too loudly, "Good to see you, son."

"Tobias," Rafael replied, and pivoted. "Have you met Eve Martin?"

Tobias's cool blue gaze raked over Eve's face. "I've… heard of her."

Rafael felt Eve stiffen beside him. He wanted to tell his father to forget what he'd heard. "Eve is my new executive assistant. I'm lucky to have her."

"It's a pleasure to meet you, Eve."

"The pleasure is mine, Mr. Wentworth."

"Call me Tobias," he said eagerly.

His father's eagerness was, in a way, kind of endearing.

Eve went on to speak with Cammie. Heads close, they were swapping stories about Micah, their "Can you believe what he did today" stories. That, too, was endearing. Rafael would need a strong drink to flush all those warm feelings away.

He looked around for his table. It was clear across the dining room—thank goodness. Audrey caught his eye and waved him over. Rafael turned to Eve. "I think they're feeling neglected at our table."

"Let's head over," she said. "Bye, Cammie!"

Cammie stared at him, a quizzical look in her eyes. "Catch you later, Rafe."

"Sure thing," he said.

Eve waved to Audrey and, possibly without thinking, caught him by the arm and led him to their table. Rafael was conscious of the gazes that followed them and the rise of whispers. Not that he minded. They could say whatever they wanted about him. But if Eve didn't like it, he didn't like it.

Audrey, Dan and his fiancé, Robert, his foreman Bill and his wife, Sandy, and Lucas were seated at the table. None of them were TCC members. Each had expressed excitement beyond comprehension when he'd extended the invitation. Lucas looked sharp in an eggplant-colored suit that Rafael's personal shopper had picked out for him. The little snot was chatting up Audrey. "You know," he said, "I graduate high school in sixteen months."

Audrey rolled her eyes. "Eat your shrimp!"

Which brought them to the shrimp arranged in delicate crystal bowls, one at each place setting. "What did I tell you?" he said to Eve as they got settled.

"Who cares?" she said. "It looks delicious."

Rafael watched, mesmerized, as she brought a plump, pink prawn to her mouth and took a lustful bite. Last night, in the shower, those lips had tightened around him and he'd had to bite into his own flesh to keep from howling.

"By the way," Eve said, "I don't hate your new car. It'll look cool when it's done."

Rafael perked up. "You can say you love it."

"Love?" She rolled her eyes. "We're nowhere near love. Let's just see how it goes."

In sudden need of a distraction, he reached for his phone and checked the alerts before silencing it for the night. Thank God, too. Among the many messages was an email from Mary Richardson that read like a hostage note.

From: mrichardson@southpointmotel.com
To: raw@ariashospitalitygroup.com
Subject: Deal
We are ready to sell. We want this to be painless and quick. No bidding wars. No middlemen. We want and expect no less than 1.5 million in cash. If you are serious, let us know by tomorrow.

Rafael let out a low whistle. It occurred to him that the thrill was in the buying, restoring and renovating. Making something old, new. Hotels, cars, it didn't matter. It was the process that mattered, and that process began with the negotiation leading to a deal.

The waiter came around for their beverage orders. Lucas was denied a beer. Eve ordered a glass of sparkling water. Rafael asked for a whiskey then returned his attention to his phone. He murmured, "Okay, baby."

Eve leaned close and whispered, "Yes?"

"Not you, sweet," he said with a low laugh. "But look at this."

He angled the screen of his phone so that she could read Mary Richardson's email. Her lashes veiled her eyes as she read.

"Wow!" She smiled up at him. "P&J were right. What are you going to do?"

"I'm going to show them just how serious I am."

He hit reply. Eve rested her hand on his; the brief contact lit him up.

"Wait," she said. "I'm sure Mary Richardson sent this same email to at least five other prospective buyers. She's tossing out bait. She's fishing."

"Here I thought you bought into her act."

"Mary is a shrewd businesswoman. No way she's letting go of her life's work for one million five."

"She's no shrewder than you."

"Well, think about it. Why would she single you out?"

"You don't think I won her over with my charm?"

"No, dear." Eve patted his hand. "I really don't."

"Let's not leave her hanging then." Rafael typed up his response, offering twenty-five grand over asking price, but only if they were willing to lock this down.

"Look good?" he asked Eve.

"Yup."

"Hit Send."

She tapped on the button then grinned at him. He melted inside. He wanted to nuzzle her neck and breathe in her light, floral perfume. He wanted to love her. Those words stunned him. He wanted to *love* her. His sweet, caramel candy apple Eve… All he wanted was to wrap her in his arms and love her.

The waiter returned with their drinks just in time. He gave his glass a swirl and took a big gulp. Eve and Audrey were laughing at something Lucas had said. Rafael set the phone face up on the table to monitor his email as the night went on, but that wasn't necessary. It chimed right away with a response.

You've got a deal.

He nudged Eve. "We got it."

Eve clapped. "Congratulations!"

From across the table, Audrey waved her cloth napkin like a flag. "What's going on? What did I miss?"

"We're the proud owners of South Point Motel," Rafael announced.

"Well done!" Audrey cried.

"Good job!" Dan said.

"Watch out, Royal!" Lucas exclaimed. "We're taking over!"

"What do you plan to do with it?" Audrey asked.

"A spa," Rafael said. "And I'm putting you in charge."

Audrey's mouth dropped. "Wait. I'm getting a promotion?"

"Get ready," Rafael said. Audrey would earn a business degree in May. She was dedicated, loyal and smart. She would make an excellent project manager.

"Oh, I'm ready! Believe it."

"Well, shoot!" Lucas said. "Can I get her job?"

"In sixteen months," Rafael said.

Lucas was skeptical. "Is that a promise? Can I get that in writing?"

"Put a high school diploma on my desk and you've got a job. It's a promise."

Lucas snapped his fingers. "Best party ever!"

"Well now!" Dan said. "While we're at it, can I get a raise?"

Everyone laughed. The Arias table, a table of misfits and outcasts, erupted in chatter. Rafael didn't hear any of it. The same few words crowded his mind: he wanted to love her.

Fifteen

Maybe it was the rush of sealing the Richardson deal or the dreamy candlelight or the intoxicating scent of flowers or the string quartet playing classical renditions of country songs during dinner, or maybe it was Rafael's hand on her knee tracing lazy circles with his thumb. Either way, Eve was feeling fine.

Not long ago, she'd had to sneak into a party at the TCC. Tonight, she was a guest of Rafael Arias Wentworth and having the time of her life. How had all of this come about? She had taken a leap of faith or two. Eve thought of Arielle. Her life had ended prematurely, but she had squeezed a lot of living into it. It might not be the worst thing to follow her little sister's example.

After dinner, Eve excused herself from the table and went to freshen up in the restroom. She swept on lip gloss and fluffed her hair. As much fun as she was having, she couldn't wait to be alone with Rafael. Although they hadn't come to any agreement, it was clear they would spend the night together. She had not yet settled into her suite, had no idea whether the bed's mattress was soft or firm, and was in no hurry to find out.

On her way back to the table, Eve bumped into reporter Sierra Morgan.

"Eve!" she gasped. "Is that you?"

"It's me!" Considering that most encounters with the investigative journalist had taken place in Eve's hospital room, her reaction was understandable.

"I almost didn't recognize you!" Sierra exclaimed.

Eve laughed, self-conscious. "Is that good or bad?"

"It's excellent! You look healthy and amazing."

Sierra looked healthy and amazing, too. The petite blonde wore a classic little black dress with no Valentine's Day frills.

"Listen," she said. "I've been meaning to reach out to you."

"Oh? What about?" Eve asked, even though she knew full well. It could only be about one thing. Sierra was dedicated to crack the mystery of the identity of Micah's father. She'd stayed on the story well after the press had lost interest and moved on to other scandals.

Sierra drew Eve to a quiet corner. "I'm sorry to say I haven't made much progress finding Micah's dad. It's not for lack of trying. I've combed through Arielle's diary and followed up on every lead."

Ah! The diary… Truthfully, it was so much more than a diary. Arielle had also jotted some notes on the big story she was working on. It involved a feud between the Langley and the Wentworth families that was as old as the TCC itself. Though everyone thought it fascinating, Eve did not. In her opinion, it fell squarely in the category of other people's business. Grandma Martin would have cautioned her to keep her nose out of it.

"I appreciate that," Eve said. What else could she say?

"I know I'm overlooking something. Just can't put my finger on it," Sierra said. "Would you be open to meeting with me sometime soon? I need a fresh pair of eyes."

"Anytime," Eve said. "Not sure how much help I'll be. I've been through that journal hundreds of times. I found some clues that led me to believe Micah's father might be here in Royal, but not much else."

In a few cryptic passages, Arielle had written of a great love and necessary heartbreak. But then, her sister had a flair for embellishment. As per numerous accounts, no one in town recalled seeing her with a man.

"Two heads are better than one," Sierra said.

"So they say."

Eve was eager to wrap things up. With all of Royal's elite within earshot, this fundraiser was not the time or place for this conversation.

"I'll be in touch," Sierra said. "Enjoy your night."

"You, too."

Sierra returned to her table. Eve, though, had an urgent need for fresh air. She exited the dining room through the beveled glass doors. Out on the terrace, a few huddled men were smoking cigars. For all she knew, Micah's dad could be any one of them. After all, the diary had made clear that he was a member of the TCC.

She headed in the opposite direction, taking the stairs slowly down to the garden. Damn, stairs were still her weakness. All those hours of PT, when would her body be back to full strength? Getting healthy, getting strong, that was her priority.

Unlike Sierra, Eve was no longer consumed with finding this most elusive of men. If he did not want to be found, maybe he was not worth finding. However, her nephew would not be a baby forever. Someday soon, he would ask about his parents, wonder about his dad. Eve wanted to look him in the eye and tell him they'd exhausted every avenue. So, she would meet with Sierra and help in any way she could, but her conscience was clear. An investigative reporter and law enforcement professionals were on the job. The man didn't want to be found. What other explanation was there?

Eve walked along the garden path and came across the bench under the magnolia tree where she and Rafael had talked that first night. She lowered herself onto it and took her head into her hands, feeling like a fool. Like that first night, the music and chatter of the party reached her. She had nothing in common with those people. Sierra had delivered a timely reminder that her problems could not be shrugged off or ignored.

Eve took her fingers to her temples and drew slow circles to ease the tension building there. She needed a clear head to think. A bullet list was forming in her mind.

- Save money.
- Rent an apartment suitable for a baby.
- Look into day care options.
- Get the okay from her doctor to regain custody of Micah.

Eve had come to Royal desperate and determined to reunite Micah with his father. At the time, she feared criminal prosecution and could see no other way forward. However, her circumstances had changed. She had landed on her feet and could handle things from here on out. If Micah's father ever showed up, great! Eve hoped the courts would see things her way and mandate supervised visits. She was not eager to entrust her one and only nephew's care to the stranger who had abandoned his mother. In the fairy-tale retelling of Arielle's life, Eve would not allow that last detail to go overlooked. Her sister's great love had abandoned her. End of story.

Rafael joined Cammie at her table and dropped into the empty seat beside her. *"Hermanita, que bella estas."*

"Hey there, Rafe," she responded, mimicking his tone. "You're looking sharp tonight."

Rafael hiked the hem of his tailored pants to show her his black leather boots. "Do you approve?"

"It's like I always say," she said. "You can take the man out of ranch country but you can't take the ranch out of the man."

"Apparently so," Rafael said. "Where is Drake? What have you done with him?"

"Sent him to the bar to get me a fresh drink."

"Text him," Rafael said. "Tell him to bring me a whiskey."

She punched him in the arm. "I will not!"

Rafael rubbed his arm in mock distress. "Ouch!"

"You missed our coffee date this week," Cammie said reproachfully.

"Quit throwing shindigs like this and we can keep to our regular schedules."

From the corner of his eye, Rafael spotted J, of P&J, zigzagging across the room toward him. *Oh, crap.*

"Finally! I got you alone!" she exclaimed. It was a funny remark coming from a woman who was forever stitched to her husband's side. "I can never get a word in without that woman running interference."

"That woman has my best interest at heart. I can't say the same of you."

Cammie tugged at his sleeve. "Who is she talking about? Not Eve, I hope."

Jennifer's face drained of color. "I mean nothing by it. It's just that we've been trying to speak with you—"

"All you ever had to do was call or stop by the guest ranch offices. Instead, you railroad me every chance you get, even when I'm trying to catch up with my sister."

Cammie wasn't done. "Eve Martin is a friend of the Wentworth family. As you ought to know, we are loyal to our friends."

"I didn't come here to cause trouble," Jennifer said. "I heard the Richardson property was suddenly off the market and wondered if you knew anything about it. That's all."

Rafael shrugged. "I guess you're just going to have to read about it in the *Royal Gazette* like everybody else."

"Alright then," Jennifer said. "You two look like you've got lots to catch up on, years of stuff, actually. I'll leave you to it."

Jennifer stormed off. Rafael grinned at Cammie and ruffled her red hair. "Damn, you're feisty."

She slapped his hand away. "You're not off the hook! Just how much time have you been spending with Eve?"

"You know I hired her."

"I know you moved her into the residence."

"You know she needed a place to stay."

"I know you're sleeping with her. That's what I know."

Rafael felt his jaw tighten. The way Cammie put it, you'd think he was doing something wrong, taking advantage of her. And yet he wasn't. For once in his life, he had someone else's interest at heart.

"Eve has been through a lot," Cammie said. "I mean *a lot*, and she's not at full strength yet. So I'm just going to make this as clear as day. If you hurt her, I'm going to hurt you."

"You already are." She had his hand in a death grip, her fingernails digging into his palm.

"There are so many beautiful women in Royal," Cammie said. "Any number of them would be glad to have you. I should know. They're blowing up my phone! Some are here tonight."

"Eve and I are friends," Rafael said. That was a thin slice of the truth. She may be the only real friend he had in Royal, but she was also the woman he was going home with tonight. "I would never intentionally hurt her."

"Your intentions mean nothing," Cammie said. "She's fragile, and you can unintentionally cause her harm."

"Eve is stronger than you think."

"Rafe," Cammie said, her tone softening, "Eve lost her sister, got accused of embezzlement, then landed in a hospital hundreds of miles away from home."

"Tell me about that," Rafael said. "What was she in the hospital for?"

Cammie frowned. "Not my place."

Rafael looked away, annoyed with himself that he

had not gotten Eve to answer his earlier questions. He was still in the dark about so much.

"It's obvious, isn't it?" Cammie said. "She has a heart condition, much like her sister, who—in case you've forgotten—*died*."

Drake returned with Cammie's drink. Rafael lingered awhile longer, making small talk. But he just wanted to speak with Eve and finally get the details of her health issues, legal troubles and financial burdens. It was time for that difficult conversation. Cammie was right. Eve had serious problems. He'd been content to distract her, and that just wasn't good enough. He could do more.

Eve wasn't at the table when he got back. He spotted her across the room, apparently having a difficult conversation of another kind with Sierra, the investigative journalist from *America* magazine. Sierra reached out and squeezed her arm as if to reassure her that the sky wasn't falling. He watched, increasingly worried, as her expression darkened.

Eve and Sierra parted ways. Sierra returned to the party, and Eve darted out into the night. Rafael got up and chased after her. The ballroom opened to a terrace, which was empty except for a few guys huddled in a corner discussing fantasy football stats. He asked whether they'd seen a woman in red. One of them pointed the lit tip of his cigar toward the stairs. He charged down the stone steps and followed the garden path. He found her seated at the bench under the magnolia tree, head in her hands. He felt frustrated that with a few words the journalist had undid all the good he had done.

"Hey!" he called out. "What are you doing out here all alone?"

She startled. "Just needed some fresh air."

"Is everything alright?" He sat next to her.

She shook her head. "I feel like I'm playing the role of the girl who is back on track. Then I get a reality check and that whole facade comes crashing down."

"You *are* on track."

"Everything is up in the air," she said. "Micah still doesn't have a father or a permanent home. And here I am in this dress, at a party. I mean…what am I doing?"

"You're doing your best," he said. "They're not any closer to finding Micah's dad?"

"No," Eve said. "And it really isn't their responsibility to find him. It's mine."

"You can't do everything, Eve."

"I doubt he wants to be found. What's stopping him from reaching out?"

"He might not know."

"But when he heard about Arielle's death, he could've at least sent flowers."

"He might not have heard," Rafael said. "Eve, you can't make assumptions like that. Wait until you have all the facts."

"I've been waiting a long time."

"I know it's not easy, darling," Rafael said. "But nothing stays buried for long, at least not in this town. They'll find him and I'll help you through it."

"That's not how it should be," Eve protested. "You hired me to do a job. You didn't sign on to be my caretaker."

"I care," Rafael said. "I'm not going to pretend that I don't. Let me help."

If he told her the truth, how desperately he wanted to protect her and make the world new for her, it would scare her to death. She'd run.

She reached for his hand and squeezed it. "Thanks, but there's nothing you can do."

He came close to laughing in her face. Save for identifying Micah's father in a police lineup, there was plenty he could do. He had the money, the contacts and the influence to get shit done. And he had the know-how to do it right.

"Do you want to leave?" he asked. "If tonight's been too much of a strain, we can go, get you to bed early."

She pulled away from him. "Don't do that."

"Do what?"

"Coddle me."

"Lady, I'm trying to take care of you."

"By taking me home and putting me to bed with a cup of tea?" She stood and faced him. Fear and frustration had left her eyes. There was fire there. "You're my lover. Can't you think of anything better?"

Every muscle in Rafael's body tensed, forcing him to move deliberately and slowly. He got up from the bench and stood facing her a moment, then with a hand to her waist walked her backward toward the magnolia tree.

"What are you doing?" she asked, slightly panicked.

Rafael didn't answer until he had her pinned just where he wanted her. "I'm going to take you against this tree."

Her eyes widened with surprise and then delight. There she was, his fearless Eve.

"Okay," she said. "Just remember I don't belong to this club. If we're caught, they'll hand you a cigar and a beer, but they'll toss me out and ban me for life."

He cupped her face and dragged his thumbs across her high cheekbones. "I would burn this club down before I let anyone mistreat you."

Eve slid her arms around his neck and kissed him hard. The heady scent of magnolia mixed with the delicate floral scent of her skin enveloped him. *He only wanted to love her.* He broke the kiss, emotion rushing to his head. He was falling, falling, falling.

Eve ran her fingers through his hair and spoke to him in a soothing voice. "Arson, huh?" she said. "Who would've thought?"

Rafael let out a ragged laugh. Eve's laugh was forced; he knew the difference. Rafael pressed his forehead to hers and she quieted down. A shudder ran through them, uniting them, and he knew this moment was more important than either of them would let on. She kissed him again, tenderly. He hoisted her up, hiked her skirt up and did what he said he would do.

Sixteen

Eve drew the pile of bills from the top desk drawer and reached for an envelope cutter. It was payday Friday, and she was grateful to have earned enough to finally start paying down her debts. She had no student loans and had always paid her credit card balance in full. However, she owed her lawyer in Miami and the medical center in Royal. Eve would likely be in the red the rest of her life, but she could get the creditors off her back. That was a step in the right direction.

Audrey poked her head through a crack in her office door. She had a date with a guy she'd met at the Valentine's Day dinner the week before, a medical student named Jamie, whom she firmly believed to be the "one."

"I'm out," Audrey said. "Any plans for tonight?"

"Physical therapy. We're going to focus on range of motion."

"Sounds hard-core," Audrey teased. "Don't overexert yourself."

"I won't. Bye!"

Audrey shut the door on her way out. Eve tore open the stiff gray envelope in which her pricey criminal defense lawyer sent all his correspondence, including invoices. She owed the firm five grand, but according to the balance sheet, she owed them exactly nothing. Zero dollars and zero cents. Eve reached for her phone and called the billing agency's toll-free number. This was the sort of mistake that would end up costing her more in the end; she just knew it. A clerk delivered the news in a flat voice. "There's no mistake. Your outstanding balance was forgiven five days ago."

"Why?"

"Our database doesn't have that information."

Eve lowered the phone. She could just call her attorney and ask. Would he bill her for that? Absently, she reached for one of her many medical bills. Her new health insurance plan had kicked in and would cover therapy and treatment going forward, but not the services she'd received prior to enrollment. She owed the local public hospital system tens of thousands of dollars. And yet…according to the notice, she owed exactly nothing. Her balance had been wiped out.

Trembling, Eve rose from her desk. There was no use calling another collection agency. She wanted answers and knew where to get them.

She crossed the hall to Dan's office. He was packing up for the day. Dan was not a chatty man by nature, and no amount of pressure would get him to spill beans of any kind. A Black man in his early forties, he wore his hair in the same buzz cut he sported during his army years. The framed photographs behind his desk proved it. Eve understood that for all her bravado, he was not the person she had to confront.

"Hey there, Eve!" Dan powered down his computer. "What's up?"

"I wondered if you could tell me what's going on with my medical bill." Although they'd run a background check on her, she didn't dare bring up her legal bills.

"Not really," he said. "Why do you ask?"

He seemed genuinely disinterested.

"My debt is wiped clean."

He patted the surface of his desk, searching for something under the blanket of scattered papers. "Lucky you."

"Here's the thing. Insurance doesn't cover services retroactively."

"Have you seen my keys?"

"No."

Her clipped tone made him look up. "Why are you mad?"

"I'm not," she said. "But I need to know if Rafael had anything to do with this."

"Why not ask me yourself?"

Rafael's voice rose from behind her. Eve shut her eyes and when she opened them, Dan looked away. In trying to avoid confronting Rafael, she had just provoked a whopper of a confrontation. There was a lesson in there somewhere.

Rafael stood out in the hall, his tie loose. He looked just as eager as Dan to end the day. Later tonight, after he met with Cammie for coffee and she wrapped up therapy, he was taking her out for tacos. A part of her did not want anything to interfere with those plans. Wasn't that the reason she'd sought Dan for answers, to leave him out of it?

"My keys were in my damn pocket all along!" Dan exclaimed. He grabbed his backpack and gingerly exited his office as if the floor were riddled with land mines. "Gotta run before traffic builds up. You know how it is."

Rafael wished him a good weekend and moved out of his way.

Eve didn't move from her post at his door. She studied Rafael's face. His expression was walled off, but he couldn't hide the truth. He knew what this was all about. Her fist tightened on the crumpled hospital bill in her hand.

"Want to talk in my office?" he proposed.

"Yes."

As soon as they were behind closed doors, she pounced. "I know what you did."

Naturally, he made a joke. "Isn't that the title of a horror movie?"

"I'm going to pay you back," Eve continued. "First thing Monday, I'll arrange for the money to be taken out of my salary in installments. We'll call it a consolidated loan."

He sat at his usual spot, the corner of his desk. "Call it what you like. You'd be paying me back for nothing."

"You paid off my bills!" Angry, she slapped the crumpled piece of paper on the desk next to him. He didn't glance at it.

"I had them forgiven. There's a difference."

"Forgiven…how?"

"My lawyers in Miami petitioned yours and convinced him to write off your case as pro bono work, considering the charges were dropped and you'd been unfairly accused. It was the only ethical thing to do."

Okay, fine! That was actually pretty decent. "What about the hospital bill?"

"Royal has a trust that covers the medical expenses of a few deserving patients each year. The board met this week, and my lawyers submitted your name for consideration."

"Then I'll pay you back your legal fees. None of your lawyers were working for free."

"They didn't work all that hard, either," he said. "It was a matter of making a few phone calls."

Eve dropped into a chair. "Is that how the rich get richer? By not paying for anything?"

Rafael raked the side of his face with his knuckles. His five-o'clock shadow was already filling in and it was only four. "We call it tapping into our resources."

She should feel grateful; instead she felt humiliated. There were only so many times you could say thank you to the same person before resentment kicked in. That was human nature.

"Would you rather I have it all reversed?"

"I'd rather we talk first!" Was it too much to ask he discuss his plans with her before putting on his white hat and charging off?

"I was going to tell you this weekend," he said, quietly. "It was meant to be a surprise."

"Rafael, you went behind my back because you knew I'd say no."

"This wasn't charity," he said. "You're not *indebted* to me or anyone. These resources exist. The average person doesn't know how to go about it and that's unfair, but it's smart to take advantage."

Oh, now she was average.

"On a side note," Rafael continued, "I could have very easily paid it all off. I've blown a quarter of a million dollars to restore a car. Money is not a problem."

"So you keep telling me," Eve said. She got it. He was filthy rich. Enough already! "How many times do I need to tell you that's not the point?"

He went around the desk and pulled a file from the bottom drawer. "This is not how I wanted to do this, but I might as well go all in."

Eve cringed. What was he getting at now?

He handed her the file. She flipped it open. Among other things it contained a science journal write-up of one Elizabeth Baer, MD, board-certified in cardiology. Eve's heart took off with a start. "What's this?"

"I've had someone look into it. Dr. Baer is the leading cardiologist with a specialty in hereditary conditions, which is what you have."

"I know what I have!" she snapped.

He toyed with a pen, waiting for her to say more. Eve dropped the file onto the crumpled bill. She wanted to scream and storm out. Instead, she held his gaze and said nothing. In her mind, she played a slideshow of all the good times they'd shared and the good things he'd done for her to remind herself that he was fundamentally a good person.

"Are you going to pass up an opportunity to better understand the disease that affects you and, possibly, your nephew?"

"Now you're being manipulative."

Rafael's demeanor changed. Those sparkling eyes went flat and that mouth, always quick to smile, was drawn in a grim line.

The hum of sadness filled her chest. "Rafael, you can't save me. You'll go broke trying."

Her life was a money pit. As soon as she cleaned up one mess or settled one tragedy there came another and another. What was he going to do? Spend all his leisure time calling lawyers and researching obscure medical conditions?

"I doubt it," he said. "Anyway, this isn't about me. Dr. Baer is one of the premier cardiologists in the world. She has an office in West Palm Beach. Currently, she's not taking new patients, but she'll make an exception. All I ask is that you think about it."

Eve's skin prickled. "It isn't fair for you to spring this on me."

"Sweet, I'm on your side."

Then why did it feel so uncomfortable?

"Think about it," he said. "I'll fly us out to West Palm Beach. Just say when."

"Rafael," Eve warned, "if you book a flight or pay for one more thing, I'm going to take you apart with my hands."

"Get into fighting shape," he said. "I'm not letting up."

Well, Eve was fed up. She stood and marched toward the door. He stopped her with one word. "Sorry."

She paused and turned to face him. He looked sorry, just not sorry enough. "Do you even know what you're sorry about?"

"For being the last card-carrying member of the patriarchy?"

Yeah. That summed it up. "I know I'm not easy," she said. "I would have put up a fight. That's no reason to go behind my back and pretend it's a surprise."

He nodded, looking properly contrite. Eve exhaled,

feeling better that she'd finally gotten her point across. Now she needed a drink of water to calm down.

She moved toward the door. Rafael called after her. "Are we still on for dinner?"

"Obviously!" She tossed the reply without breaking her stride.

He'd promised her authentic tacos. If he thought he could piss her off and deprive her of tacos all in one day, he could think again.

Seventeen

Cammie poured him a cup of coffee, and they went out onto the back porch. Micah was napping, and the house was quiet when Rafael had arrived. His sister looked relaxed, barefoot and wearing jeans. He lit the cigar Drake had offered him and sat on the steps. The setting sun traced a fine red line over the horizon. Rafael wouldn't share this with anyone, but a part of him was rooted here in Royal. When he wasn't fending off rumors, railing against the TCC, or clashing with Tobias, he felt settled and calm in a way he never did anywhere else.

Cammie got him up to speed on the latest happenings in town, particularly the conversion of the Carrington ranch into a student training facility. Gabe Carrington had been his closest friend in high school. It was too bad that he'd relocated to New York City with his wife,

Rosalind, shortly after Rafael had returned. Cammie talked and he smoked and nodded. From time to time he said, "Right." After his argument with Eve, he couldn't focus on anything. He just wanted to sit here, smoke his cigar and not give a damn about the world at large.

"Isn't that great?" Cammie asked.

To which he replied, "Sure, I'll contribute."

"Are you even listening?" she asked.

"Sorry. I might have spaced out."

She slipped off the porch rail and came to sit beside him on the steps. "What's the matter? Is it Tobias?"

Rafael shrugged and let out a long stream of smoke. "It's Eve. She's mad at me."

"But you two looked so happy the other night!"

"Well, she's not happy now."

"What did you do?"

"I had her debt wiped out, both legal and medical."

Cammie took another sip of coffee, mulled over his words. "That's actually pretty nice."

"I thought so."

Cammie blew a strand of red hair away from her face. She had freckles across the bridge of her nose. "What's the problem?"

Rafael stared into the distance. "I didn't tell her what I was up to. I just handled it."

"That's a very Tobias move."

"It was meant to be a surprise."

"A bouquet of flowers is a surprise," Cammie said. "A weekend getaway is a surprise. Paying off debts is a what-the-hell type moment."

"In a way, this is your fault."

"In what way?" Cammie said. "I asked you to be

careful with her, not take over her life. You see the difference, right?"

"If I'd asked for her permission, she would've said no."

"You may look like your mom, but there's a lot of Tobias in you."

"Don't say that."

"Too late!"

She went back to sipping her coffee. Rafael drew from his cigar. "Fuck… That was a Tobias move."

"Thank you!" Cammie cried, nearly spilling her coffee down her T-shirt. "So, how did it go down? Did you two fight?"

"We exchanged words."

"Did she end things?"

"No!" Rafael snapped. He couldn't even stomach the idea. "We're getting tacos later."

"Tacos? Sounds like you're cool."

"We're not. You didn't see the look she gave me."

And Cammie hadn't heard the tone of Eve's voice, filled with outrage and pain. He knew he'd gone too far.

"Do you mean all of this is because of a look she gave you?"

"All of what?"

She drew a circle around his face with the tip of a finger. "The forlorn look, the sorry little frown, the woe-is-me attitude."

"Stop!"

"*You* stop!"

They were different people when they were alone together, behaving mostly like annoying teenagers. Even Drake had remarked upon it. The best part was that they were okay with it. Rafael understood they were actively making up for lost time, and it was nice. Jennifer Carlton was right about them. They had a decade's worth of stuff and more to catch up on.

"She called me manipulative," Rafael confessed.

"Damn!" Cammie exclaimed. "Eve packs a punch. Who knew?"

Rafael dropped his cigar in the ashtray and leaned his head on his sister's shoulder. "I fucked up."

Cammie pat his cheek. "Yeah, you did."

"What should I do?"

"Okay. What I'm going to say is going to blow your mind. Ready?"

"Go on."

"You apologize."

He pushed away from her. "I already apologized!"

"Alright, then. Now you wait."

"Wait for what?"

"For her to come around."

"Is that all? I need an action plan."

"Your action plan got you into this mess."

"Your job is to knock sense into me and tell me what to do."

"And your job?" she asked.

"Punch the boys who make you cry."

She laughed. "I'll go with that."

"I've got your back, baby cheeks."

"Quit calling me 'baby cheeks'!"

Cammie didn't have baby cheeks anymore, but she did once and that was all that mattered. The nickname was hers for life.

"You want advice?" she said. "Don't follow the Tobias playbook. Ask yourself, 'What would Tobias do?' Then do the opposite."

"Good advice," he said. In the back of his mind, he couldn't help but think they were being hard on their dear old dad. Tobias's marriage to his late third wife had been, by all accounts, a loving one—as hard as it was to believe.

"Speaking of Tobias, how are your lunches going?"

"They're going," Rafael said. "The trick is to avoid the hot topics. Once I get there it's all sports all the time."

Cammie pat his back this time. "He *is* trying, you know."

"I know," Rafael said quietly. "I'm trying, too. At the same time, I want to tell him to fuck off and go to hell. It's weird. You know?"

"Oh, I know. Trust me."

They fell silent. Rafael looked to the sky. He had so much shit to figure out. Right then, a scratchy sound came through the portable intercom Cammie carried around with her. Micah was stirring. Drake's low voice followed. He made a soft cooing sound. Cammie cut the volume and put the monitor aside.

Rafael glanced her way and caught her silly little grin. "What's that?" he asked. "The state-of-the-art baby walkie-talkie?"

Cammie shrugged. "You'd be surprised to learn how much equipment a baby needs just to stay alive."

"They need love, too, I'm guessing."

She brightened. "Love, too. Yes."

"Hermanita—" he reached out and squeezed her hand *"—no quiero verte lastimada."*

Her smile went crooked. "I don't know what that means."

"It means—"

"No," she said, shaking her head. "I don't want to know, either."

Rafael let out a sigh and resumed staring out into the distance. "We're screwed up, aren't we?"

Cammie dropped her head on his shoulder. "Royally screwed."

First thing Monday morning, Rafael had a conference call with a team of engineers. The guest ranch was going solar. It wasn't as easy as it sounded. There were permits to secure and the matter of retrofitting new panels on old construction. Still, he would not be deterred. It was good for the environment, good for the bottom line and good press. There would always be a media outlet eager to publish a story on the hospitality industry's efforts to cut its dependence on fossil fuels. He wanted his company to be part of that story.

"This is my top priority," Rafael declared.

Right then his cell phone buzzed in his breast pocket. It was a call from Eve, which was odd. Normally, when they were in the office, she'd swing by or buzz the intercom. Since their fight last Friday, nothing was normal between them. They'd gone out to dinner and spent most of the weekend together, but each night she'd returned to her suite. Cammie had advised him to wait for her to come around. What if she never did?

Rafael hit mute on the conference call and answered his cell phone.

"Are you busy?" she asked.

"Not too busy for you."

"Good. I need help testing a theory."

"Where are you?"

"The Belleview Inn."

He liked where this was going. "To be clear, you're referring to the internationally known Sex in an Inn Theory?"

"That's the one," she said. "I bet if we tried really hard we could disprove it. What do you say?"

"I say give me ten minutes."

Rafael was giddy when he wrapped up the call with the engineers. Top priority or no, something even more pressing had come up.

Eve had booked a deluxe room and the Do Not Disturb sign hanging from the doorknob boded well for him. He knocked. She came to the door in lingerie, a delicate, pink matching set. Cotton-candy pink, bubblegum pink, stretched over lush caramel breasts. Her hair was wavy and loose past her shoulders. She looked him over. "You're overdressed for this experiment."

He returned the favor. "Give me a second. I'm having a moment."

She smiled. "Hate to rush you, but there's a draft and I'm freezing."

The tension that had been building in him all weekend broke. It was relief, more than anything else, that made him reach for her. The door slammed shut behind him. He buried his face in her neck and pinned her to him, hoping to hide the fact that his whole body was trembling. Their standoff had lasted three nights, three nights of waiting and, honestly, going a little crazy.

She was laughing. "I knew that would do it. You're obsessed with keeping me warm."

He kissed her at the spot that always made her shiver. "Now I'm obsessed with making you hot."

Kissing her hungrily, he blindly guided her from the

foyer to the bedroom. They tipped onto the bed together. He ached to suck on her chocolate nipples through the veil of pink lace. But Eve slipped her fingers in his hair, like she loved to do, and brought his mouth to hers.

"Hey," she said sweetly.

He crushed her full lips with his kiss until he tasted sugar—and then a knock on the door. Rafael pulled away with a groan. This was fucking déjà vu.

"I ordered chocolate covered strawberries," Eve explained. "Sorry, I passed on the champagne."

Her wide brown eyes were filled with such eagerness it broke his heart. "That works for me."

He rolled out of bed, grabbed the goods, settled the tab and sent room service away. He found a condom in his wallet. Eve was sitting up when he returned. Her hands were linked behind her head.

"Don't get too comfortable," he said.

"Alright." She crawled the length of the bed and kneeled at the edge.

He tore off his clothes. She reached for him, asking for another kiss. He kissed her mouth then dipped his head, dragging his lips along the scalloped edge of her bra. "This stays on." He slipped a hand in the waist of the lace underwear. "This comes off."

"You're a demanding man, Rafael Arias."

But am I the man you love?

The words took up so much space in his mind that he came close to saying them out loud. To silence his mind, he covered her body with his and kissed her like the first night. His mouth trailed down her body, tracing a line straight down the middle until he met with liquid heat. Eve's fingers curled and tightened in his hair. Her back arched with each stroke of his tongue, but no sounds escaped her. That didn't sit well with Rafael. He licked and sucked and scraped her swollen bud with his teeth until she gasped and cursed his name. Only then did he pull away and crawl up the length of her body, triumphant. Her lips were parted, inviting, but he dipped his head and whispered in her ear. "That's not very nice what you just called me. I've been very good to you."

She pressed a kiss to the corner of his mouth. "And very bad."

Laughter rumbled through him. "Take the bitter and the sweet."

"Yes, please."

Rafael hooked an arm under her knee, eager to be inside her. She planted the palms of her hands to his chest. Though panting, she managed to deadpan. "Missionary? Really?"

Rafael laughed outright. "Darling, I don't make the rules."

He slipped on the condom. She snaked her arms around his neck. "So you keep saying."

His laughter rolled to a stop. The anticipation of pleasure tugged at every muscle of his body. "I need you. Hold me close."

Eve wrapped her legs around his thighs, taking him deep inside her. Rafael closed his eyes. He could not describe this feeling, scorching hot yet achingly sweet. That was Eve, thrilling him with every touch, every uttered word, every glance, every kiss. They rocked in smooth motion until crashing in pleasure. For a long while, they lay breathless and spent in each other's arms. Eve buried her face in his chest. Rafael stroked her back and whispered into her hair. "Sweet love, thanks for coming back to me."

* * *

Now that he had such wonderful memories at the Belleview, Rafael wondered, shouldn't he buy it? He asked Eve whether it was a good idea. She bit into a strawberry and shook her head. "This isn't Monopoly. You don't have to buy up every square you land on."

"It just feels so good being here with you." He wasn't serious about buying the place. After all, he'd checked and the inn with all the local charm belonged to a multinational conglomerate. But he wasn't kidding about how it felt to be here with her, like coming home.

"It always feels good," she said. "No matter where we are."

"That's true."

He drew her into his arms and held her close while they watched the midday news. Outside the temperature had dropped, and the weather reports predicted a dusting of snow. The program ended with a story of Gabe's ranch, now a training facility. Rafael told Eve about Gabe, his high school years and early childhood. He told her about his mother who died and the bullish way Tobias had reentered his life. "He took me in and gave me his name. It was the right thing to do, but I'd just lost my mother and didn't want to lose the name that linked me to her. Tobias didn't ask me or anyone else how we felt about it. He just did it. Cammie's mother took off, pissed. It was a shit show."

At some point, Eve had reached for the remote control and silenced the television. She rested her head on his chest and just listened. He was really killing the mood that she'd worked hard to create. Rafael was sorry about that and everything else.

"It's classic Tobias to take action for the greater good

without taking into account anyone's feelings on the matter. I'm sorry I did that to you."

"You're not off the hook," she said. "I'm still angry for the way you went about it. You can't just push me aside and take action on matters that concern me. I won't stand for it."

"I'm on notice," he said. Rafael hadn't tolerated Tobias's BS. He expected no less from her.

"Good," she said. "I *am* grateful, though." She circled her arms around his waist and pressed her body closer to his. "I asked you here to tell you that."

"You could've just sent flowers."

"You know what? It was a toss-up between pink peonies and pink panties."

"You made the right choice."

"And you've lifted a great burden off my shoulders. I don't know how I could ever—"

Rafael brought a finger to her lips. He did not want her to carry on about finding ways to repay his kindness. "Please don't finish that sentence."

"I need you to understand," she said. "I depend on the kindness of strangers for just about everything. It makes me feel small. I wish you had met me before."

"When you ran with the 30 Under 30 crowd?"

"Yeah," she said with a laugh.

Eve reached for her phone on the nightstand. She tapped on the browser and pulled up an article by a Miami business magazine. She was recognized for setting up a database for a South Florida nonprofit organization. In the accompanying photo, her hair was pulled back in that tight bun she used to wear and her expression was fixed. Rafael kissed her forehead. "I think I like you better now."

Eve pinched the photo to expand it and studied it awhile. "I think I do, too."

"Have you given any thought about the doctor?"

He hated himself for bringing it up, but it was too important. Her health was on the line.

"Yes, I have," she said. "I decided it wouldn't be smart to turn down the opportunity out of spite. Although I'm tired of doctors and hospitals, I have to stay healthy for Micah."

Rafael held his breath. Eve was vacillating, and if he said the wrong thing, he could tilt this the wrong way.

"So, we can go whenever you're free."

"Seriously?"

She shrugged. "What harm can it do? If the office is in Palm Beach, it'll probably be like visiting a day spa."

Rafael doubted that. Not one to procrastinate, he grabbed his phone off the nightstand and dialed Dr. Baer's office. They scheduled a 10:00 a.m. appointment for Friday. "We'll fly straight to West Palm. When you're done, we'll head down to Fort Lauderdale. I'd love it if we could spend the weekend at my hotel."

She plucked a strawberry from the crystal bowl on the tray beside her, swiped it in the chocolate dip and brought it to his lips. "I'd love it, too."

Eighteen

Eve should have been elated to board a private jet to Florida. But the bliss of returning home was clouded by the true purpose of their visit. They were not headed to a resort hotel where she'd slip on a bikini and lounge by the pool. That would come later. Their first stop was a doctor's office where she'd slip on a backless gown and stretch out on the examination table only to be told she had six months to live. That's how it was going to go down; Eve was sure of it. Doctor visits didn't end with positive, uplifting news—not in her experience, anyway.

"What's going on in your mind?" Rafael said. "I'd pay to know."

Eve let out a sigh. "Just a little nervous."

Seated across from her, Rafael tapped the tip of his boot to the pointy toe of her shoe. "Where's my fearless Eve?"

Fearless Eve? She did not know who that was. Fear had her in a cage, mental and physical. Early on, her physical therapist had said her recovery could go faster if she would only push herself. "You're afraid," he'd said. "You can do more." At the time, she was afraid she might lose her footing and fall on her face, pass out and land in the hospital, or lose her life like Arielle. The same wheels were turning now. She was afraid to hope only to stumble into bitter, bottomless disappointment once again.

Rafael was watching her intently. Eve shifted in her seat, feeling uneasy. He patted his thigh and mouthed, *Come here*.

She shook her head. "Can't unfasten my seat belt. We haven't reached cruising altitude yet. Captain's orders."

"Don't worry. I'll keep you safe."

She sprang from her seat, abandoning the cold leather for the warmth of his lap. He kissed just below her ear. "What's wrong?"

Everything was wrong. Their first weekend getaway was for medical reasons. There was nothing sexy about it, but this was her life. Eve took a trembling hand to her throat. She pushed down a sob. Rafael cradled her in his arms. He let her cry without interruption. He did not try to console her. He simply let her get the toxins out. Eve surrendered to the torrent of tears, too strong to manage or control. It felt so good to be supported. All through her ordeal she had received help and assistance from government and nonprofit organizations, from the medical staff at Royal Hospital, even from strangers like Cammie and Sierra. What she had not had was a shoulder to cry on. She'd held Micah, but no one had ever held her.

Rafael stroked her hair. "I'll be brave for you," he whispered. "You can rely on me for this."

She pressed a palm to his chest. "I am grateful."

"I don't want you to be grateful," he said. "I want you to get well for selfish reasons."

She caught a flash of worry in his eyes. This relationship was meant to be light and fun. His role was to bring light to her life. She was not meant to darken his. Those were the terms of their agreement. Now she worried something else was at play, and she had to address it head-on.

She freed herself from his tight embrace and sat upright. "Rafael, may I ask you a direct question?"

He leaned his head on the headrest. "Go for it."

"What's happening with us? Are we catching feelings?"

He peered at her with one eye shut. "What? Catching…fireflies?"

She may be a straight shooter, but Rafael was a master of deflection. *"Feelings,"* she repeated. For good measure, she spelled out the word.

"I know what feelings are, Eve." He slipped a hand under her loose cotton blouse and rolled his knuckles along the grooves of her lower spine. "Do you feel that?"

"I'm serious!" she cried, although the back rub felt really good.

"You're too serious."

A moment later, when the flight attendant offered her a cashmere blanket and poured them both French roast coffee, that all felt good, too.

"I need you to focus on *feeling* better," he said a while later. "That's all that matters right now."

Eve agreed wholeheartedly, so why did her heart

tank? She dipped a biscotti into her coffee and pulled up her mental to-do list, the one she'd drafted the night of the fundraiser then promptly abandoned the moment Rafael had pinned her to the magnolia tree. She revisited it point by point, adding one more:

• *Don't catch feelings for this man.*

Dr. Baer was a reserved woman, somber and soft-spoken, with steel-gray hair and keen gray eyes. Eve spent three hours in her office undergoing a battery of tests. Dr. Baer reviewed the results and delivered somewhat hopeful news. "This is not a severe case. There is no reason you can't manage your symptoms now that you are aware of your condition. I am prescribing medication. I recommend moderate exercise and a plant-based diet. We'll follow up in six months at which time we can discuss other treatment options."

Eve was reluctant to accept the news on face value. "My sister died of this. Giving birth was too much for her heart and she couldn't recover."

She saw Arielle in her hospital bed, her life seeping from her body. She knew hours before her sister passed that she had lost her.

"You are not your sister," Dr. Baer said. "Remember that."

Rafael was in the waiting room when Eve stepped out. He said that he had gone out to handle some things while she was busy, but she suspected that he hadn't gone far. He looked a little bent out of shape. She rushed into his arms. On the ride to Fort Lauderdale, she repeated the doctor's words.

"Sounds like we got good news," he said. "Now we can relax and celebrate."

Eve could only think of sleep. It had been a grueling day.

When they arrived at the hotel, Rafael was greeted like an emperor. His staff seemed genuinely thrilled to have their boss back, and that was a rare and beautiful thing. Everyone, from the valet attendant to the general manager, wanted his ear. It took a while to make it through the lobby. She thought they were in the clear when they got on the elevator. Eve wrapped her arms around his waist and leaned on him. A woman raced across the lobby, heels clicking on the terrazzo floor. "Hey, stranger!" she called out. "Hold the elevator!"

The woman crashed into him, and judging by Rafael's reaction, he did not need a shield this time.

"Claudia!" He pulled the brunette into a hug. "It's been a long time."

"It's been ages! I'm happy to see you, but I'm so mad at you. Where have you been?"

"Good old Texas," he said, reviving his twang.

Claudia laughed and tossed back a lock of hair. "You're a Texas boy at heart."

"You may be right about that," Rafael said. "What are you up to?"

"It's Tatiana's birthday," she replied. "We're all meeting at the bar for drinks. Join us! It'll be like old times."

Rafael declined the offer. "Eve and I have plans."

Claudia opened wide eyes and took in Eve as if just now realizing that she and Rafael were not alone in the elevator. "Ah! Is this Eve?"

Rafael nodded. "Eve, this is Claudia, an old friend."

Claudia took a step back, disappointment tugging at the corners of her mouth. Even so, she managed to sound cheery. "Hey! Nice meeting you."

"Likewise."

Claudia got off on the twentieth floor, leaving behind the scent of her perfume. She and Rafael rode up to the penthouse floor, which was reserved for private residences. Rafael kept an apartment in Fort Lauderdale. Although he loved the Miami property, he said it could get rowdy. Fort Lauderdale was chill enough to feel like home. A home with room service, turndown service, laundry service and any other service you could think of including an in-room massage.

Eve couldn't put Claudia out of her mind. With the dimple in her chin and twinkle in her eyes, the glossy brunette looked vivacious and fun. If he'd gone off with her, he would've had a better time. Now that she'd seen him in his element, she understood there was little chance of him catching feelings for her. He would sooner catch a cold. With her sad stories, health issues and teary fits on private planes, she was nothing like Claudia. Rafael could cross out every item on her laundry list of problems, and she still wouldn't be like Claudia. The thought made her sad and tired.

Rafael gave her a tour of the penthouse. It was white, stylish and a little sterile. None of that mattered when you factored in the sweeping ocean views from every room. The bedroom was serene with a large bed dressed in white and few other furnishings. Rafael suggested she lie down awhile. Eve crawled onto the bed and sunk her head into a stack of pillows. All her negative thoughts dissolved into darkness.

* * *

She woke up hours later in a darkened room. Disoriented, she shuffled out of bed and stumbled down the dimly lit hall to the living room. She was bothered by the reigning silence. Had Rafael abandoned her yet again? No…no… He wouldn't. And yet her heart didn't settle until she saw the ruby-red tip of his cigar. He was out on the terrace that wrapped around the penthouse. Actually, he was in the sunken Jacuzzi out on the terrace, head back, blowing smoke into the night.

Eve squeezed her eyes shut and took a breath. Why had she freaked out, thinking he'd flown her all this way just to abandon her? Come to think of it, she'd been one erratic hot mess this entire trip. They were far from Royal, far from the responsibilities that she'd left there. She could maybe leave those cares behind for a day or two.

Eve headed back to the bedroom. She rummaged through her luggage until she found the bikini that she had ordered online and paid extra for overnight delivery in the hopes this weekend would have more to offer than a series of doctor visits. When she joined Rafael out on the terrace, he grinned up at her. The cigar in one hand, a tumbler with amber liquor and ice in the other, dark hair slicked back, he looked relaxed.

"Look at you," she said.

"Look at *you*," he tossed back. "How are you feeling?"

"Rested." She walked over to the edge of the hot tub and dipped a foot, the gurgling bubbles tickling the tip of her toes. "Listen. I need a favor."

"Anything."

"Whatever you do, don't let me think too much. Not tonight. Or this weekend. I need to get out of my head."

"Alright, darling," he said. "Whatever you need."

Eve exhaled, releasing the pressures of the day. "What are you drinking?"

"Whiskey." He raised the glass. "Want it? Come and get it."

"No, thanks," she said. "I'll have an iced tea."

"We make excellent mocktails here," he said. "How does a *nojito* sound?"

"Sounds delicious."

"I'll order," he said. "You'll have to get the door. My state of mind is very obvious right now."

"I'll get the door," Eve said. "I don't have those problems."

He took a drag from the cigar and looked at her through a screen of fragrant blue smoke. "But you cause them."

Eve bit back a laugh, loving the way his gaze skimmed her body.

"Is that new?" he asked, gesturing to her bathing suit.

She raised her hands to her hips. "You like?"

"Very much," he said. "You left the tag on."

"Oh!" She looked down and wondered how she'd missed the tag dangling between her breasts. Rather than pull it off, she reached behind her back, unfastened the bra top and let it fall to the side.

Rafael nodded appreciatively. "I was going to rip off the tag, but your solution works, too."

Eve didn't stop there. She looped her thumbs around the waistband of the bikini bottom and, with a little shimmy, lowered it to her ankles and kicked it aside.

"My God," Rafael groaned. "Eve, do you want to stop my heart?"

Eve eased into the water. "I need you alive for what I have in mind."

He dropped the cigar into an ashtray and reached for her. The strength of the whirlpool made his task easy. Eve drifted to him and soon she was in his arms, wet skin to wet skin, mouths thirsty only for each other. His hands were everywhere. "Don't think of anything except how this feels."

It felt amazing, absolutely amazing. She wrapped her legs around his hips, clinging to his body and his words.

"Don't think of anything except how much I want you," he said. "Promise?"

"Promise."

It was a promise she broke almost instantly, as she took in the twinkling city lights in the distance, the swirl of warm water all around them and the night that pulsed just for them. Could she be dreaming?

Rafael was too perceptive to let her thoughts wander. "Where have you gone?"

She pressed her forehead to his. "I'm here with you."

"Good." He kissed her again. "I can't think of anything but you."

Eve could feel his heart pounding in his chest. A current of fear moved through her just as strong as the water churning around them. She could not fall in love with this man, and yet she was dancing dangerously close to the edge. To break the mood, she splashed him with water. His grip tightened around her waist and he pulled her under.

The "nojito" came later. Then dinner. Then lying in bed, talking about nothing in particular while Rafael played with her hair. The next morning, Eve slept in while he met with his staff. In the evening, they took a boat and navigated the Intracoastal Waterway to one of Rafael's favorite seafood restaurants. At a rickety wood table, he pounded stone crab legs with a mallet and explained how their pail of "peel and eat shrimp" was better than standard-issue country club shrimp cocktail.

"If you've peeled it, you've earned it," he explained with a straight face. "It's that simple."

"Is that right?"

Rafael leaned back and joined his hands behind his head. "I'm telling you. It's all about the good old elbow grease."

He wore a plain white T-shirt and a pair of soft slouchy jeans. He looked so good, the crisp white cotton contrasting with his golden brown skin. This quick trip had revived him, too, apparently. She commented on it, and he offered her a sad smile. "I'm torn between two cities. Royal is who I am. My roots are there. For better or worse, my family is there, too. Fort Lauderdale built me, made me the man I am today. Most people think I started out in Miami, but that's not true. It was here. Now I'm not sure where I belong. I've got a lot to figure out."

Eve understood. She was in the same boat, so to speak. Facts and figures had forever been her passion, but working alongside Rafael had given her a different perspective. She liked the hands-on nature of his work and enjoyed watching an idea unfold from conception to realization.

She unpeeled a rosy Gulf Coast shrimp. "I'm not sure what my next step will be."

A wrinkle creased the space between his brows. "You have a home at Arias Hospitality Group—always."

That was very reassuring, but staying on as his assistant was not her endgame. It was too soon to seek a promotion. Gradually, she could take on extra projects.

"Was your dream to work in finance?" he asked.

"No," she said. "I went to business school to start a business of my own."

"You wanted to be an entrepreneur."

"Not really," she admitted. Her dream was far less romantic. "I wanted to make my first million before turning thirty. Starting a business is the fastest way to do that."

Rafael took a swig from a chilled bottle of beer. "Do you know what happens when you turn thirty?"

She flashed a smile. "I haven't reached that milestone."

"I'll tell you," he said. "You stop caring about bullshit milestones."

Eve stopped caring about a lot of things. The rest of the weekend flowed by without a worry or a cloud in the pale blue Florida sky.

Nineteen

They arrived in Royal fairly early on Sunday afternoon, only four o'clock local time. Rafael knew Eve was anxious to see Micah and proposed they swing by Drake's ranch on their way home from the airport for a quick visit.

Drake greeted them with a grin at the door. "A little weekend getaway to Miami, huh?"

"It wasn't like that," Rafael said. "We had something to take care of."

"We never made it to Miami," Eve said, as if it made a world of difference. "We mostly stayed in Fort Lauderdale. Rafael worked the whole time."

"The whole time?" Drake looked him over. "Is that how you got your tan?"

"What can I say? I'm a whistle-while-you-work type of guy."

"I bet."

Cammie came down the stairs with Micah. "Hey, you two! What a surprise. I wasn't expecting to see you this weekend."

"I couldn't wait to see Micah," Eve said.

"Here he is," Cammie said. "He just woke up from a nap."

Eve went over to the sofa and, once settled, Cammie placed Micah in her arms. She cradled him close to her heart. He squealed with delight and burst into tears.

"He's fussy," Cammie said. "It's time for his bottle."

Drake had another idea. "I know what he needs."

Cammie and Drake parted in different directions. Cammie returned with a bottle of warm milk. Eve took it from her and slipped the nipple into Micah's pink little mouth and rocked him as he started to suck vigorously.

Drake returned with a small yellow teddy bear and handed it to Rafael. "Here you go, Rafe, my man."

"What's this?" Rafael asked.

"Yellow Bear."

The toy was the size of his hand. "Does it have a name?"

"That's his name—Yellow Bear."

"Original," he murmured.

"When it comes to kids, simplicity is key," Drake explained.

"And you're an expert now?" Rafael said, incredulous.

Cammie intervened. "Rafe, quit arguing and dangle Yellow Bear above Micah. He likes to grab at it while he's feeding."

Rafael sat next to Eve on the couch and did as instructed. He dangled the bear before Micah's eyes. The baby reached up to grab it.

Cammie slipped out her phone. "I'm taking a picture. You three look like a family!"

Eve shook her head. "No, we don't."

"Kinda do," Drake said, settling comfortably in an armchair.

Cammie snapped her fingers, demanding their attention. "Eyes on me. Smiles. Good. Got it!"

Eve had smiled for the photo, but quickly lowered her head. Rafael wondered what he was missing.

Cammie studied the photo she'd just taken and nodded appreciatively. "A damn good-looking family, too!"

Rafael felt his jaw tighten. Was Cammie projecting her hopes on them? Her dream had always been to have children, preferably with Drake. The tragedy was his bighearted sister had not found a willing partner in the man that she loved. But from what he'd gathered from their recent talks, Drake had done a full 180. It was all thanks to Micah. But the little one wasn't a miracle worker. Unlike Drake, Rafael wasn't going to suddenly change his outlook just because a cute baby had dropped into their lives.

He brought it up on the drive home. "Eve," he said, his eyes on the road. "May I ask you a direct question?"

"Go for it." She was less jittery now. Time with Micah always calmed her down.

"What are your long-term plans for Micah?"

"Oh." He felt her staring at him, but he could not meet her eyes. "You're asking because Cammie put you on the spot back there. Sorry about that."

"I'm asking because I want to know."

Eve had come to Royal in search of Micah's father. They'd yet to find him, but he was sure they would. When that day came, what sort of arrangement would they come to? She was very attached to her nephew. He couldn't imagine her just turning him over.

They stopped at a light, and he reached for her hand. "Sweet love, talk to me."

She very slowly withdrew her hand from his. He knew then that he had missed something back at Drake and Cammie's place. Somehow, he'd upset her. For the life of him, he couldn't think what that could be.

They drove the rest of the way in silence. He removed their luggage from the trunk of the car and loaded the elevator. They rode up to their floor. When they passed her door, she slowed to a stop and called out to him. "Rafael, wait." There was an edge to her voice and he knew, whatever the argument, he'd lost.

"I'm going to regain custody of Micah," she said. "Just as soon as I reach my therapy goals and the doctor signs off on the paperwork."

Rafael cleared his throat. "Have you considered waiting until you find his father? There's no rush, really."

"I'm not waiting. He could go screw himself for all I care."

That edge in her voice was anger mixed with resentment.

"Are you worried about Cammie and Drake?" he asked. "Because they'll keep him for as long as you need. I think Micah's done them a world of good."

"It's dragged on long enough," she said. "They'd only signed on to foster for a short time. I expected to be done with PT by now, but the doctor overseeing my therapy is strict and won't sign off until I hit every single goal."

"Cammie doesn't mind. Far from it."

"I can't outsource my nephew," Eve said. "He's my responsibility."

"So what is your plan?" Rafael asked. "How soon is soon?" Even to his ears, his questions sounded curt.

"As soon as possible."

Eve surprised him with an elaborate plan that involved her moving out, getting her own place, securing day care and, because it was worth repeating, moving out.

"Eve, I thought you were happy here with me."

"I am." She went to him and slung her arms around his neck the way she liked to do when they went for long walks on the grounds and no one was around. "But I have responsibilities I can't shrug off. Please understand."

"You don't have to move out to do that."

She laughed off his comment. "Rafael, there's no room in your life for a child! You know that."

He had one more direct question for her. "Are you ending things with me?"

She shook her head. "Not really."

"It's yes or no, Eve."

"We can always see each other," she said. "It probably won't be the same."

He didn't want things to change between them. He liked it as it was. Something sharp was clawing at him inside. "You never shared any of this with me. When were you planning on telling me you wanted to move out?"

"I don't have any definite plans as of yet. My physical therapist thinks if I do well within a few more sessions, he'll talk to the doctors. And maybe I will ask

Cammie to keep Micah a week or two longer, until it's all settled."

"A week or two?"

"Rafael, I can't let your sister raise my nephew so you and I can live free."

"No one is saying that—"

She stepped away from him and started pacing around furiously. "The only reason I let it go on so long is because I was afraid. I worried that I'd black out at a parking lot, leave him on the hood of another stranger's car and start the whole vicious cycle over again."

"I understand all of that, Eve," he said. "I knew this day was coming, but we could have talked about it."

This was rich coming from him, considering his past behavior. But Rafael felt something slipping from his fingers. It made him desperate.

"Rafael, this isn't about you," she said with exasperation. "This is about Micah. You don't understand what it's like to have children or care for children. It's like you said—you're not wired that way."

"And I've told you why."

"Or maybe it's just a choice you've made," she said.

"It is my choice," he said unapologetically. It was a choice that he had a right to make. If Cammie was right and he was more like Tobias than he'd wanted to think, it was probably for the best.

"Exactly," Eve said. "You're the lone wolf or the black sheep or whatever else you call it, and it suits you. But I don't have a choice. My sister died and left me her son. I have no other family, and I have to do right by him. There are no other options for me. I'm not like Claudia."

"Claudia?" Rafael was genuinely confused. "What does she have to do with this?"

"You belong with someone like that," Eve said. "When I saw you with her, it all made sense."

At the moment, Eve was talking nonsense. "You saw her for all of five minutes."

"You know what I mean."

"I don't. If it's that clear-cut and we're so compatible, why aren't we together? She's single and so am I. Why aren't we riding off into the sunset together?"

"I don't know," she shot back. "Maybe you ought to consider that instead of spending all your time, money and resources trying to fix me."

Rafael drew a breath. "Look, we're exhausted," he said, as diplomatically as possible. "Let's head inside, shower and grab something to eat. We'll talk about this with cooler heads."

"No," she said. "I need some quiet time. I think I'll stay here tonight."

"Are you sure?"

"Uh-huh." She searched her purse for the keys that he'd never seen her use. He followed her into her suite and left her suitcase inside the door.

"May I come by and check on you later?"

"I'll be asleep."

Rafael didn't know how he managed to keep on standing when really he was in free fall. This was how it was going to end; he was sure of it. She would close the door on him, and there would be no way back.

Twenty

Hovered over her bathroom sink, her breath shallow, Eve was in the throes of an anxiety attack. It was over between her and Rafael. She'd understood it the moment they returned to Royal. Their joyride had come to an end.

She had Rafael to thank for her hard-won independence. He'd given her the job and even arranged for her to see the doctor. So now she no longer had any excuses. Each time she visited with Micah she felt guilty for not being more present or somehow doing more. Drake's comments about the Miami getaway had stung. He was only kidding and she knew it, but it didn't feel right to leave her nephew with Cammie while she and Rafael took off for weekend escapes.

In general, Eve wasn't fascinated with Royal's storied past, its feuds and drama handed down from generation to generation. However, it was well-known that

Tobias Wentworth, Rafael and Cammie's father, had a solid reputation of being a ruthless, stingy, hard-ass businessman. In contrast, his kids were generous to a fault, giving without ever asking for anything in return. Eve loved them both, fiercely, but she could not rely on them forever.

She and Rafael were locked in the roles of generous benefactor and damsel in distress. They couldn't carry on like this. At some point, he'd resent her or she'd resent him. He would certainly want someone on his level, and that wasn't her. The imbalance of power and privilege was just too great. Maybe it wasn't Claudia, either. It was his choice to make. There was no doubt in her mind that the generous thing to do was to cut him loose.

So now what? How do you break up with your boss? Was there any guidance on that? Office affairs were the worst. They seldom worked out. When things fell apart, you were stuck with your ex as a colleague or boss. Rafael was a good, decent man. He wasn't going to make things difficult. In the end of the day, he'd stuff down all his feelings and put on a friendly, impersonal mask. He'd call her Ms. Martin, and not in a sexy way. He'd duck out early on Fridays so there wouldn't be any awkward run-ins at the elevators. He'd be a perfect gentleman. He just wouldn't be her lover.

It began as early as the next day. The office suites were unnaturally quiet. Eve assumed Rafael had stayed away on purpose. Even though it hurt her, she was thankful. They needed a reprieve. Later, they could pick up again and carry on as before. For the moment, they needed space.

At lunchtime, Eve picked up a salad and ate at her

desk. She didn't have an appetite and ended up pushing her plate aside and dropping her head on a stack of files. There was a hole in her heart that nothing could fill. She might have stayed like that, despondent and desperate, right up until quitting time if Sierra Morgan hadn't called. She wanted to meet for drinks. "We could talk and go over Arielle's diary, like we discussed."

"Yes. Absolutely."

"How about we meet at the Colt Room at five?"

The Colt Room was a wine bar at the TCC. Eve was beginning to think that all roads in Royal really did lead to the country club. "Meet you there."

At four thirty on the dot, Eve grabbed her keys and headed out. There was still no sign of Rafael. She did not hear his voice down the hall or his rambunctious laughter. Not a peep. Nothing. It gutted her. Was this her future? Rolling around like an empty shell, going through the motions of daily life, all the while knowing that there was someone out there who could make her days bright? If only her hands were free to grab the one he extended.

Rafael spent the morning at the Richardson property. Mary Richardson very graciously showed him around and led him through a point-by-point inspection. She showed him the tiles that were missing from the roof, demonstrated plumbing issues and pointed out the squeaky floorboards. Rafael followed along with a heavy heart. He would've liked to do all of this with Eve. It wasn't part of her job description to follow him around, but he had grown accustomed to having her at his side. He couldn't stop thinking of the observations she would have made or the private jokes they would have shared when Mary Richardson wasn't looking. She would have no doubt drafted a quirky list.

He knew it was over between them and did not understand why. They were good together. She thought he belonged with someone like Claudia. Meanwhile, he couldn't picture her with anyone else. Who could love or care for her better? Just the thought of it pissed him off.

But what about Micah?

It had been so easy to overlook this point because Micah had been safe and sound with Cammie. Realistically, that couldn't go on forever. Eve said she couldn't outsource her nephew, and he realized that was exactly what he had hoped she would do.

"Are you alright?" Mary Richardson asked.

"Oh sure!" He accepted a glass of sweet tea when they reached the end of the tour.

"You're not having second thoughts, are you?"

"Hell no!" He checked himself. "Sorry, ma'am."

"That's fine," she assured him. "I curse up a storm, too. It's just that we're counting on the money."

"I promise you I'm not withdrawing my offer. We are going through with this."

"Good to hear."

"What are your plans for the future?" Rafael asked.

She reclined in a rattan chair on the porch. The motel was as much her home as her business. It was her whole life. "We have our eyes on a lake house."

"Sounds nice."

"It's time for us to walk away," she said. "We put so much work into this place and expected our kids to take over. Turns out: they have dreams of their own. We held on as long as we could, waiting for one of them to change their minds. Too long, really. We just couldn't walk away. At some point you have to ask yourself—do you own a business or does the business own you?"

"That's pretty deep for a Monday morning," Rafael mused. "Maybe too deep for me."

"Nah," Mary said. "You're a smart guy. Just think about it. You wouldn't pour all your money into one project. Well, that's what we did. We put all our energy into this motel and seldom took a day off. The goal was to secure the future. Meanwhile, the future is passing us by. Understand?"

"I think I do."

"What are your plans for this place?" Mary asked. "Are you going to tear it down?"

That wasn't his nature. For someone who swore up and down that he didn't believe in looking back, he liked to preserve the past. The motel was built at the turn of the last century. The architectural details made its charm. He would restore it and bring it back to its old glory. He made that promise to Mary, adding that he would invite them back for a visit when it reopened as a spa.

Mary nodded. Wisps of gray hair escaped her loose braid and glistened in the sun. "Looks like we picked the right man."

He'd stayed for lunch, and it was two in the afternoon when he took leave of the Richardsons. Rafael still wasn't ready to return to the office. He was not ready to see Eve again, to see the truth in her eyes. Eve was determined, a trait he normally liked. Except now she was determined to destroy the world they'd built together, and there was nothing he could do about it. Thankfully, another option came up.

Manny called and held up his phone to a car engine to let him hear it purr. "You'll want to hear this in person," he said.

"I'm on my way."

He tore through the streets, taking back roads to avoid traffic. He arrived twenty minutes later and Manny went through the production of unveiling the car. The old clunker was now a *Camaro*, with a new engine and its original electric-blue paint. He swept a hand along the grain of the leather seats, realizing with sadness that every time he admired the buttery caramel color, he would think of Eve.

Manny must have misread the crumpled look on his face. "Bro, don't get emotional!"

Rafael waved him off. "It's nothing."

"Where's prom date?" he asked.

"She's at work."

"That's too bad," Manny said. "She would've gotten a kick out of this."

"I think so, too."

"Bring her next time. She was good people."

"We'll see." Rafael looked around for a distraction. He tested the horn.

Manny came over and leaned against the car, hands in his pockets. "What happened? Are you two going through it?"

Rafael glanced at him and caught his knowing look. "Is it that obvious?"

"You look like someone stole your lunch money, your puppy and your brand-new bike."

"That bad?"

"Oh, yeah!"

"There's nothing I can say. I'm not really sure what happened."

One minute they were happy, the next she was making plans to move out. Frankly, he felt blindsided.

"That sounds about right." Manny went over to the mini fridge, pulled out two bottles of beer, cracked them open and handed him one. "Come on. Let's go sit outside and not talk about it."

Rafael pushed out a dry laugh. "Yeah. I'd like that."

Twenty-One

Eve sank into a leather banquette, across from Sierra. They had opted to take their drinks to a table for optimal privacy. Sierra looked smart as usual, her tousled blond hair framing her face, her eyes shining with intelligence and curiosity. But dread rose up steadily in Eve's gut like bile.

"There's a reason why I asked to meet with you at this bar," Sierra said.

"Really?" Eve said. "I just thought everyone liked to hang out at the TCC."

"True," Sierra said with a knowing smile. "There are other spots in town I like to go to when I'm not working. But this bar in particular, the Colt Room, does it have any significance for you?"

"None," Eve said, confused. "Why would it?"

Sierra produced Arielle's diary, face open. Eve

took in the scrappy handwriting penmanship that she had made fun of back when she and her sister were in school. Her heart seized; she had to look away. Combing through the diary, discussing her sister, all of it was painful. It was necessary if they would have any hope of finding Micah's father, but it wasn't fun. This wasn't an exciting mystery she was aching to solve; it was a tragedy that pained her to relive. Honestly, her motivation was gone. Finding Micah's father was no longer her focus. The more time passed, the less it mattered. Her name had been cleared, and no judge would separate a child from his one surviving relative. She would have liked to tell Sierra to let it go. Eve was convinced the man didn't want to be found and with that arose a conviction deep within her that her family was complete and perfect without him.

Sierra tapped on a note in the margin of a page: one word, *COLT*, with little hearts drawn around it. She flipped the page. "Here it is again, underlined."

"I must have missed that," Eve said. In her feverish search for clues in her sister's diary, it shocked her that there were dots she had failed to connect.

"We can take it literally," Sierra said. "Maybe she took up riding. Was she a horse person?"

"Not that I know of," Eve said. "But when in Texas, right?"

Sierra laughed at the joke, but it came across as a professional courtesy more than anything else. "I thought it might have something to do with this bar."

Eve nodded agreeably. "Okay."

"There's happy hour on weekends. Maybe she came here once, had a good time and wanted to come back."

"That's possible, I guess."

She took in the brassy opulence of the Colt Room. It did not look like the type of place her easygoing sister would frequent, but then again, what did she know? It was obvious she did not know her sister as well as she thought.

"Are you alright?" Sierra asked, closing the diary.

"Oh, sure," Eve said. "This is difficult, but I'm okay."

"Is that all?" Sierra was ever the inquisitive reporter. "It's just the other night, at the fundraiser, you looked so happy."

"It was a fun night." Eve took a sip of lime soda to better evade Sierra's eyes.

"Sounds like both Martin sisters found love in Royal," Sierra said. "You and Rafael Wentworth make a cute couple."

Eve nearly choked. "How do you know? Did he say something to you?"

Sierra went red in the face. "It was in the *Gazette*."

Eve was glad they weren't seated at a bar height table; she would have fallen off her stool. "In the *newspaper*?"

Sierra pulled out her phone, tapped the screen a few times and pulled up a local newspaper's gossip column. Beneath the headline ROYAL'S NEW POWER COUPLE?, a photo of her and Rafael at their table at the Valentine's Day fundraiser, heads close, reading from the same phone. The camera caught them smiling conspiratorially. Other than that, there was nothing salacious about the photo—thank goodness. What if the photographer had caught them under the magnolia tree? That would have been a whole other story. Eve scanned the column. There was a quote from Jennifer Carlton. "Those two are inseparable! For sure they are a couple."

Heart sinking, Eve returned Sierra's phone. The image, though, was imprinted in her mind. She and Rafael looked so damn happy. What a cruel prank! It was as if the universe were taunting her with the image of the life she would never have. She drummed the tabletop with her fingers. "Great," she murmured. "Just great."

"It's a...great photo," Sierra offered.

"I know what it looks like—"

Sierra raised her hands. "No need to explain. I'm sorry I brought it up."

She looked so uncomfortable, Eve felt obliged to diffuse the tension. "What were you saying about the Colt Room? Maybe there is something to it."

"I thought so," Sierra said. "Except before you arrived, I showed Arielle's photo around. None of the bartenders or waiters remember seeing her."

"I'm not surprised," Eve said. "She would have preferred grabbing a beer at a college bar than sipping Chardonnay at the Cattleman's Club."

She was about to add that she and her sister were not the country club type, but the words never cleared her throat. She'd met Rafael here. Today she felt at ease, meeting with an acquaintance at the club for a drink. As much as anyone could feel at ease when their heart was splitting in two, obviously.

"I've been over it and over it," Sierra said. "It's a minor detail, but if feels big. You know?"

"May I ask you a question?" Eve said.

"Certainly."

"Why are you so...dedicated to this?"

Sierra took a moment before offering a carefully crafted answer. "I came to Royal to write about this club, its secrets and old ghosts. It's great and all, but your little nephew grabbed my heart. I was there from the beginning, you know. I was one of the first people on the scene when Cammie Wentworth found the little guy on her car."

Eve sat upright, but her inner walls were crumbling. Her imagination pieced together the scene when Cammie and Sierra discovered Micah abandoned on the trunk of the Mercedes. She was close to tears again, but this time she steeled herself. The time for crying had passed. If Sierra wanted to dig further, she would help her.

Eve racked her brain. "There's something else…"

Sierra leaned forward, eager. "Go on."

"Micah's middle initial is C," Eve said. "No middle name. Just an initial. We're a small family and no one's name starts with C." She had asked Arielle about it, but her sister had brushed her off. "I can't imagine it stands for Colt. That would be…ridiculous."

"Would it, though?" Once again, Sierra pulled out her phone. It seemed to have all the answers. Her prior research on the country club had not focused on the swanky bar. As to be expected, everything about the TCC, even a wine bar, had a story. "There's this blog I followed back when I was researching the club. It's chock-full of tidbits… Okay! It says here that members of the TCC would gather in the Colt Room for drinks after voting."

Eve imagined the members gathering to vote on a "no fun allowed" clause. She reached for a cocktail napkin to hide her smile. Rafael's words would forever make her laugh. That was something she would take with her.

"Well, now!"

Sierra's exclamation pulled Eve out of her Rafael-induced haze. "What is it?"

"Listen to this—one of the founding members is named Colter Black."

"That's an unusual name."

"There's more." Sierra perked up. "Colter Black donated the funds to build and stock the bar."

Colter... Eve turned the name over in her mind. Micah Colter Martin.

Sierra was positively giddy. "So much for my horse theory."

"Unless Colter Black has a great-grandson by the same name who crossed paths with Arielle while she was in town, I don't know what to make of it."

"You leave that to me," Sierra said confidently. "This is what I do. If there's a young Colter Black out there, I will track him down and swipe him for a DNA sample myself."

"It may come to that," Eve said dryly. "It still irks me that he hasn't made any effort to reach out."

"There's a chance he doesn't know."

"Now you sound like Rafael."

"Well then." Sierra set down her phone and picked up her wineglass. "He sounds like a pretty smart guy."

As luck would have it, Eve pulled into the residence parking lot only moments after Rafael had slipped into his reserved spot. He cut the engine and sprang out of the low sports car. She stayed put, her hands gripping the steering wheel. He looked disheveled. When he got closer, she saw that his eyes were bloodshot. This was her handiwork. She had managed to turn a joyous, outgoing man into this—whatever this was.

He held the car door open for her and helped her out. They stood facing each other for a while. She resisted the urge to reach up and smooth his hair.

"We made the papers," she said. "They published a picture of us at the fundraiser. They asked if we are 'Royal's New Power Couple.'"

He shrugged. "I wouldn't mind it if it were true, but we're not a couple anymore, are we?"

Eve didn't care so much about the headline. She couldn't get the photo out of her head. The photographer had captured an intimate moment. Her expression was one of a woman pampered beyond belief, content, not wanting for anything, happy at last. It had frightened her to see it, and it made arguing that they had never been a couple that much harder.

"Sweet love, come here," he said quietly.

It was a plea and she could not resist. Eve drifted to him. Even now, she could not keep her hands off him. She reached up and smoothed his hair. Slipping her hand down to his neck, she massaged the tension there.

His hand fell to her waist and he drew her even closer. "Couldn't we…just once maybe?"

A smile broke from the inside out. "Yes. Maybe just once."

His kiss was tender. When he pulled her into his suite a while later, and they frantically tore at each other's clothes, his kiss was still tender. She stepped out of her dress. He sunk to his knees, pressed his face to her flank, murmuring, "Eve, sweet Eve." He kissed her from freckle to freckle, connecting the dots. She bent forward to meet his mouth. Then all tenderness subsided, giving way to relentless desire. The world quieted around them and no sounds existed beyond their sharp breaths, the moans that escaped their lips and later the cries that spiraled out of her. As the sparks of their desire died down, Eve curled up to him in bed and listened to his heartbeat. That silk thread of tenderness returned, wrapping itself around them, tying them together.

Later, Eve slipped out of bed and quietly got dressed.

"Don't go," Rafael said.

"If I stay, I'll never want to leave."

"Stay," he said. "Move Micah in if you like. There's plenty of room in here."

She looked around for her shoes. "Yes, but there's no room for a child in your life. A baby is not a part-time gig or a sidehustle. You have to be all in. Does any of that sound appealing to you?"

Rafael propped himself up on an elbow. "I don't have to become Micah's dad to be in your life."

"Do you want to be anyone's dad, though?" she asked. Since they were on the topic, she might as well go there.

He raised his chin. Even in the half-light, she could see defiance stirring in his eyes. "Is that a deal-breaker?"

"It is," she said. This ordeal had made it crystal clear. Having lost her family, she wanted a second chance. Her life was wrapped around Micah, and there was room in her heart for more. "I know with most couples this conversation doesn't happen until months into the relationship. And I know it's not fair to dump all this on you like this. But it's worth asking if we even want the same things. If not, maybe it's best we end it now before anyone gets hurt."

"I want you," he said, without even a trace of doubt.

"I want you, too," she said. "Rafael, I'm so glad I

met you. You've changed my life. I'm sorry I wasn't up front about my plans, but this was never meant to get so out of hand. From the day we met I thought you understood. The only reason I'm in town is because of Micah. If his father doesn't show up, I'll probably move back to Florida."

Despite the encouraging leads that Sierra was pursuing, Eve was committed to follow her own plans all the way through.

Rafael fell back onto the pillows and ran a palm over his face. "Now you want to move out of state," he said, speaking into the dark.

"Florida is home. There is nothing for me here."

"Nothing?"

She caught the mix of hurt and betrayal in his voice. She rushed to apologize and botched that, too. "Look, in a few weeks, you'll be over it. It'll be in the past."

"You think a few weeks will change how I feel?"

He couldn't conceive of it now, but she was right about this. He would likely move on to another project, something else neglected and timeworn to restore and make new again. He would forget her eventually—maybe not in a few weeks, but in time.

Rafael tossed back the sheets and got out of bed. Pulling her close, he stroked her cheek. "Sweet love… Nothing that you're telling me is real. Right now, it's just you and me—and we're happy. Why are you looking for the quickest way out?"

"Try to understand," she pleaded. "That's not what I'm doing."

Eve was reeling. How could he possibly think that?

"Yes, it is," he said. "Trust me. I'm an escape artist. I've done it more times than I can count."

Eve felt some shame when she walked out on him moments later, almost proving that he was right. Back at her suite, she poured herself a glass of water and went to sit at the bay window. Time passed and gradually, night slipped into day. In the distance, light scattered from behind the pine trees. This was the first sunrise she had witnessed in Royal, and it brought new clarity. She could not stay here much longer. She and Rafael would never resolve their differences. They could not go on like this, falling into bed only to fight afterward. Now that she was debt-free and had a little money saved up, there was no use putting off the move. In the morning, she would get in touch with a real estate agent who specialized in short-term rentals. It was time to get her plan in motion.

Twenty-Two

On Saturday, Rafael met his father for lunch. Tobias was seated at their regular table, a chilled glass of beer before him. The old man looked good, solid and healthy. His trim beard had a silver sheen. He was perusing the menu, although Rafael was sure he would order the rib eye with a side of baby vegetables to balance things out, a lazy attempt at lowering his cholesterol. Rafael just couldn't do it. He couldn't join him, order the burger and fries and start talking about the big game, whichever game that was. He couldn't pretend that everything was fine when it wasn't.

Rafael strode over to the table. "Let's go."

Tobias looked up from the menu. His blue eyes, piercing at times, were hazy with confusion. "Where are we going?"

"Never mind. Just come with me."

The waiter arrived looking just as confused as Tobias. "Anything I can help you with?"

"We're not staying." Rafael pulled out his wallet and left a twenty to cover the beer. "We'll be back same time next week."

Tobias followed him outside and said, "What's gotten into you?"

"We're going to get some real food."

"There *is* real food here," Tobias objected hotly. "The best steak in Royal, if you ask me."

"Well, I'm not asking you." His car was where he'd left it. The valet had not yet taken it to the remote site. He retrieved his key. "Come on. We'll take my car."

A moment later, Tobias slid into the passenger seat. "Mind telling me where we're headed?"

"Nope."

Rafael drove in silence to a part of town he was sure Tobias hadn't visited in a while, not since he was courting his mother, anyway. The cobblestone streets were narrow. Most of the signs were in Spanish. The homes were modest, and the businesses could only be described as mom-and-pop shops. He pulled up to an eatery. Tobias dutifully followed him inside. Rafael ordered the special: *Lonche de carnitas*. The beer was served in plastic cups. They took their food to a table in the courtyard, hidden among terra-cotta pots spilling with ferns. Much to his surprise, Tobias dug in with delight, red-faced with joy.

"It's good, right?" Rafael asked.

Tobias grunted his approval. "Damn good."

"Maybe every once in a while we could come out here for lunch instead."

"I'd like that," Tobias said, looking very much like

a man who just found a winning lottery ticket stuck to the sole of his boot.

"Good." Rafael took a bite of his sandwich and savored the fresh baked bread, grilled beef and onions. He washed it down with a swig of cold beer. It was a cool day, but Rafael felt as if his head was on fire.

They finished lunch in blissful silence. Tobias wiped his mouth and said, "You want to talk about whatever it is that's making you this crazy?"

"No," he replied, avoiding Tobias's keen gaze. All trace of confusion was gone.

"Are you sure?" Tobias asked.

Rafael slumped back into his seat. He had to get it out or it would eat him inside. No amount of comfort food was going to do the job. "Eve doesn't want to be with me. She thinks I have a problem with her nephew."

"*Do* you have a problem with her nephew?"

"Not at all," Rafael said. "He's a fine little kid. I love the little guy."

"So?"

"She figures she'll be raising him someday. Someday soon."

"Ah!" Tobias said. "Cammie will miss the little guy. She's grown to care about him a great deal."

Rafael nodded. "I know."

"I guess it can't be helped," Tobias said.

"I'm afraid not," Rafael said. "Eve is making plans that don't include me. She doesn't think I'm up for it."

Tobias took a sip of beer. "Are you up for it?"

"Are you just going to repeat the last thing I say?"

"That's my strategy," Tobias said evenly.

"It's a good one," Rafael admitted. "What kills me is that she's right. I don't think I'm up for it."

"Do you love her?"

Something ripped inside Rafael, the veil that had been keeping his emotions separated, everything nice and tidy. "Yeah, I love her. All I want to do is love her. But do I see myself buying a house on a hill and settling down like Cammie and Drake? No, I don't. Hell, I don't even know what city I want to live in. I'm not that guy. I told her this on day one. I'm not wired for it. No offense, Dad." The word *Dad* had dropped from his lips like a stone, but it was rolling around out there and he couldn't take it back. "No offense," he continued, his tone softer, "but you and Mom did a number on me."

"Let's be honest here," Tobias said. "It was mostly me."

"Yeah." Rafael laughed. "I don't know why I looped Mom into this. She's a saint."

Tobias nodded gravely. "No argument here. I was a fool to have messed that up."

"You were young," Rafael said, surprising himself. His saint of a mother had often used this argument in the hopes of easing Rafael's resentment. It had never worked before.

"My mistake," Tobias said cautiously, "was not getting it right the first time. I've lived a long time, and now I know how important that is. There is no going back. The most you can do is make amends. But there is no repairing the damage done. I know. I've been trying."

Rafael looked up at the sky. There was just one lone cloud drifting by. "I know you've been trying, and I appreciate it. I do. I know I don't show it, but why else am I here in Royal? I have roots here, and I can't just walk away."

Tobias gripped his napkin. He held Rafael's gaze,

even though tears turned those blue eyes to clear pud-
dles. Rafael felt uneasy. Pain and resentment momen-
tarily loosened its grip on his heart, allowing him to
breathe freely for the first time in his life. He could very
well pass out from the influx of oxygen.

"Do you want my two cents?" Tobias asked.

Rafael shrugged. "I'm not talking to hear myself
talk."

"If you love her, then you have to support her. This
must be difficult for her. The baby is not her child. She
didn't ask for this responsibility, but she's showing up
for it. That's a beautiful thing. The fact that she doesn't
want to burden you is also selfless. The question is,
what are you going to do?"

"Have you been meditating or something?" Rafael
asked good-naturedly. "Suddenly you are so profound."

"Ah…" Tobias sighed. "I'm alone a lot. I've got lots
of time to think."

Just then Rafael received a text message from Manny
that instantly cheered him up. He glanced at Tobias.
"Want to go for a joyride?"

"Son," Tobias scolded, "what did you go and do
now?"

"You'll find out soon enough." Rafael rose from the
table. "Are you coming?"

"Hell, yeah!"

"Alright, old man. Let's go."

"Watch yourself, young man," Tobias said, as he followed Rafael out of the restaurant. "Who you calling
old?"

Over a lonely lunch at her kitchen counter, Eve learned
that Royal's rental market was booming. The real es-

tate agent had laughed at her laundry list of demands. Eve wasn't trying to be picky. It made no sense to move Micah from a palace to a shoebox. There was no matching Drake's ranch in comfort and style, but a bright space in a safe neighborhood wasn't too much to hope for, right? Wrong. Apparently, the chances of her finding a decent apartment at a decent rate were slim.

When she got off the call with the agent, she noticed an unread text from Cammie inviting her out for a stroll in the park with Micah. Eve rushed to accept. It was a fresh Saturday afternoon, and she needed an excuse to get out. She had nowhere to go. Although Cammie and Drake had always welcomed her with open arms, she didn't feel comfortable showing up at their home at all hours of the day.

Cammie was waiting for her by the fountain when Eve arrived at the park. Eve plunged her hands into the stroller and pressed her cheek to Micah's warm chubby face. He cooed in response. The rush of love was so overwhelming and comforting that she couldn't imagine giving it up for anyone or anything. The feeling confirmed that she was on the right path and doing all the right things, for her and her nephew's sake.

Eve, Cammie and Micah proceeded unhurriedly along the trail that circled the park. Cammie shared stories of Micah's attempts at eating green foods, mostly pureed organic peas that she brought fresh from the farmer's market. She showed Eve a short video of Micah shoving his hands into a bowl of green paste. Ordinarily, Eve adored these stories complete with the multimedia images. Sometimes, Cammie would send her a short video first thing in the morning and that alone would brighten her day. Today, however, she could only listen in silence, feeling increasingly uncomfortable.

Cammie was devoted to Micah 110 percent. Eve hadn't given this full consideration. She believed her ties to her nephew were the strongest because, after all, they were blood relatives. However, she could no longer write off Cammie's contributions as mere charity. Her attachment to the little boy was real. Not only real, it was deep. It was pure. It was love. For someone who had arrived in town knowing no one, Cammie had been God sent.

Eve stopped midstride. It took Cammie a few more steps before she realized that she was walking alone and talking to herself. She turned around and said, "Are you okay?"

Eve nodded, but she suddenly didn't feel so good.

"Oh, God! You're not well!" Cammie sprang into action. She steered the baby carriage with one hand and reached out for Eve with the other. She guided them both to the nearest park bench and tapped her back as if she were a baby about to spit up her peas.

"I'm okay," Eve said. "Really. It's just… I have something to tell you and it's not easy."

Cammie's expression fell. It wasn't long, though, before Eve caught the glint of steely Wentworth determination in her eyes. "Don't worry," she said. "Whatever you have to say, I can take it."

Such a strong family! Cammie's reaction was so similar to Rafael's. Eve could hug her.

"I just wanted to say thank you."

"Is that it?"

"For now." Their eyes met, and a current of understanding passed between them. "From the bottom of my heart, I really want to thank you. I owe you and your brother a debt of gratitude that I simply cannot repay."

"Oh, Eve, I don't know about that. You crash-landed into our lives and made everything better. Maybe I should be thanking you for the privilege of caring for Micah. Do you know how long I wanted a child in my life? This was a blessing for me. It made me think. It made me realign my priorities. It made me grow. Every day I wake up grateful for this opportunity. Plus it opened Drake's heart. We're now planning on starting a family of our own. We couldn't be happier. I know it won't last. I know…" Her smile was uneven, betraying what it cost her to make that statement. "Could we not talk about it just now? It's such a nice day."

"How about some ice cream?" Eve proposed, trying to recapture the levity they'd lost. "There's a truck over there."

She pointed at the string of food trucks only steps from where they were sitting. Cammie was game. "Sure. Let's do it."

They walked to the trucks and back. Micah started to fuss, and Eve didn't hesitate. She scooped him out of the stroller and bounced him on her lap.

Cammie cheered. "There you go! I knew you could do it."

"I guess therapy helped."

"It also helps to trust the process. You're going to be fine."

Cammie received a text message. She tapped on the screen and her jaw dropped.

"What is it?" Eve asked.

"I can't believe my eyes!" Cammie exclaimed. "Look at this!"

Between Micah and the melting ice cream cone, Eve had her hands full. Cammie angled the phone so she could see the photo on the screen. Rafael and Tobias in the restored Camaro, top down, wind in their hair, both men looking tan and flashing matching smiles. Cammie started to type an answer then stopped. "We can do better." She tapped on the camera app and switched to selfie mode. "Let's send a photo back."

"Let's not."

Eve shifted out of the shot. Cammie caught her with her free hand as she'd done moments earlier. "Don't run! You're part of the family."

That sounded lovely, but she doubted it very much. Rafael had sent the photo to his sister alone, closing the circle. She was not in the loop. Eve started to protest, but Cammie would not be deterred. "ONE! TWO! THREE! Everybody say cheese!"

Eve held up Micah and hid behind him like a coward. The irony wasn't lost on her. She was using Micah to hide from Rafael, in selfies and in real life. Cammie snapped the photo, examined it, grumbled something about needing more sun, added a filter and sent it on its way. Eve shuddered at the swoosh sound the phone made to confirm the message had been sent. Then Cammie returned her attention to the photo of her brother and father. "This isn't a small thing."

Eve agreed. That Rafael had brought his father to Manny's car shop was a truly amazing thing. It was his happy place. She had felt so honored when he'd brought her there.

"I had to work so hard to get these two together. It was tough enough to get them both in the same state. I would have never arranged for them to ride in the same car out of fear they'd kill each other."

"They look like they're having fun," Eve said.

"That is the miracle!" Cammie cried. "They've been at each other's throats for years. To see this... It's incredible. My family was shattered. My every effort to piece it back together was met with resistance. Rafael is just as stubborn as my father. For years, I sent him letter after letter, pleading with him to no avail. He said he was focused on his future and had no interest looking back."

Funny. That was how Eve felt at the moment, focused on her future. There was no looking back, no time to think of what might have been. This wasn't stubbornness, not in her book. She had good reasons to stay the course. But that picture of Rafael smiling with his father told a different story. He had yielded and, apparently, it had worked out for the best.

"What made him change his mind?" Eve asked, curious.

"The tenth anniversary gala of admitting women members into the TCC."

"No kidding!"

Cammie nodded. "Why does that surprise you?"

"It's just... He talks so much *shit* about the TCC."

Cammie laughed. "That means nothing! He's from Royal. The club has a special place in his heart. My father and I announced the official launch of our nonprofit that night by awarding college scholarships to kids of first responders and hospital workers. Rafe came back to stand by us. I was so moved. It showed me his heart, you know? And his friendship with you—"

"Has he talked about me?" Eve interrupted.

"I badgered him for information," Cammie said. "He cares about you, no doubt about it. Seeing you two together is one of the best things to come of this."

Eve's first instinct was to deny, deny, deny, but that would be a waste of time. "We won't be together for long."

"No?"

"I don't see a future for us, so there's no point dragging things on forever."

Cammie's eyes widened. "You don't see a future?"

"No, I don't," Eve said resolutely. "We don't want the same things out of life. It's more important to be with someone with whom you're aligned rather than not."

"Trust me," Cammie said. "Speaking from experience, I totally understand. It's a shame, though. It really is. I'm going to put the blame squarely on my brother. He's a tough nut to crack."

"It's not like that." Micah put a fistful of Eve's hair in his mouth. She struggled to free her curls from the baby's iron grip. "He's been wonderful."

"Yeah…he can be wonderful, but he can also be set in his ways. Then again, he can surprise you, like today." She held up the phone, indicating the photo. "As his meddling little sister, I'm going to ask you to give him a chance. Don't write him off completely. He may need time. He may need an infuriating amount of time. But he's so worth it. Look at us. Our relationship is way better than I could have ever hoped. I have a big brother again!" Cammie's nose turned red. She dabbed at her eyes with the corner of Micah's blanket. "Can you believe it? I have a big brother who wants to be in my life. And today my brother and my dad are out on some crazy joyride in a vintage I don't know what."

"A 1969 Camaro."

"Look how much you know!" Cammie exclaimed. She studied the picture. "And look at that interior! Love the color. It's beautiful."

"It is," Eve said, close to tears. "It's beautiful."

Twenty-Three

"This is a hell of a nice surprise!" Cammie exclaimed. "My big brother picking me up for a spontaneous outing. You're lucky I was here. I work from home most days, so I can care for Micah."

Rafael was glad she was game. He'd showed up at the foundation headquarters around noon with all of fifteen minutes' notice. She came skipping out of the building, wearing a sharply tailored business suit and swinging a shapeless tote bag. Rafael was leaning against the Camaro's passenger door. She gripped him by the shoulders and shoved him aside.

"The car!" she cried. "I get to ride in it, too!"

"Nothing but the best for my baby sister!"

She ran around to the driver's side. The top was down. "Look at it! How luxurious!" She ran her hands on the leather seats. "I love this tan color."

"Not tan," he corrected. *"Caramelo."*

"Ah, yes! It's gorgeous."

"Glad you like it."

"Give me the keys," she said. "I'm driving."

Rafael didn't see that coming. "Hell no!"

"Oh, hell yes!" she fired back. "I'm driving or I'm not going anywhere."

"Fine!" He tossed her the keys.

"Hop in!" she squealed.

Rafael did not hop in. He watched with amusement as Cammie got settled behind the wheel and adjusted the rearview mirror. "How can I get me one of these?" she asked.

"You have to know someone who knows someone."

"Luckily, I know you. How soon can we get the ball rolling?"

"The sooner the better," he replied, and reluctantly slid into the passenger seat. "Then you can drive your own car."

Cammie pulled out her phone. "Let's take a picture and send it to Tobias."

"Oh, please!" Rafael moaned.

"Hey! I want this moment immortalized." She held up her phone. Rafael leaned close and held up two fingers. She snapped the photo, sent it along.

"Can we get back to business now?" Rafael said impatiently.

"What business?" she asked. "It's just lunch. Chill, already."

"We're not going to lunch."

"What?"

"We are *not* going to lunch."

Cammie scrunched her brows in confusion. "You

pick me up at noon on a weekday and you are not taking me to lunch? How do you figure?"

"We're going to run an errand."

"There better be food involved with this errand because I'm starving. I left behind a totally fine BLT wrap in my mini fridge."

"Fine!" He caved for the third time. He wasn't in any particular hurry. He'd cleared his calendar for the afternoon. But he was afraid that he would lose his nerve. "We're on an important mission. If you want lunch, swing by a drive-through."

"I know just the one." Cammie fired up the engine and put the car in gear. "I feel cheated, though. Dad said you took him out to get the best steak sandwiches, and I demand no less."

"I'll take you to my spot some other time."

"Where are you taking me?" she asked, while skillfully zipping through traffic.

Rafael couldn't rush the answer. When they arrived at the burger and barbecue joint, he proposed they sit at one of the picnic tables.

Cammie was ecstatic. "Now you're talking!"

They'd picked a table in the shade. Rafael pounded ketchup out of a bottle and covered his fries with the stuff. Cammie sipped her milkshake through a paper straw that wasn't up to the task. She set the cup aside. "What's the big hurry?"

"I asked you to come out with me because I need your help."

"Okay."

"It's delicate."

"Uh-huh."

"I'm not stepping onto your turf or anything—"

"Yes?"

"Eve and Micah—"

"Oh, God…"

The breeze picked up and tousled her red hair. Rafael's heart melted for her. "You know where I'm going with this?"

She reached out to squeeze his hand. "Eve and I had a talk."

"You did?"

"Yeah, well, not really. We have an understanding."

"Oh?"

Cammie nodded briskly. "Nothing definite, of course."

"And you're okay with it?"

"To the extent that I can be."

"There's nothing definite on my end, either," Rafael said, reassuring her the best he could. "I want to be prepared in case she'd like to bring Micah over for a night or a weekend or more."

Cammie straightened up. *Ohhhhhhh.*

"That 'oh' long enough?"

"Not in this case! Tell me more." She reached for the milkshake again and sucked hard on the straw.

"She doesn't think there's room for the baby in my life. I need to do something concrete to show her. See what I mean?"

"I see."

"I was thinking about getting one of those basket thingies for Micah to nap in."

"A basket? So Micah is like a baby Moses drifting down the Nile?"

"What are you talking about? I see it on TV all the time! It's in every movie."

"You mean a bassinet," Cammie said. "Micah has outgrown those things. You need something sturdy and solid."

Rafael knew better than to argue with her. She was the expert in this case. "See?" he said. "That's why I need your help."

"First, I have a question."

"What's that?"

"Did you try telling Eve how you feel?"

"She knows how I feel."

"That's not what I asked," Cammie said. "Did you ever tell her in a sentence how you feel about her. Did you say 'I love you, Eve'? 'I can't live without you. Your problems are my problems. Your burdens are my burdens. You don't have to walk this road alone. I'm here for you.'"

Rafael looked down at his ketchup-smothered fries.

"Did you say any combination of those things?"

Rafael remained silent.

"Just to be clear—you did not tell her you loved her."

"I didn't! Okay?"

"It's not okay!" she cried, scaring away a crow. "Damn it, Rafe! You're doing it again."

"Doing what?"

"A Tobias move!"

Rafael pushed his food away, suddenly nauseous. He was a lost cause.

"You see what I mean, right? You skip the tedious communication part and leap straight into the take action part. You can't do that, buddy! You have to talk first, communicate your feelings and then together take proper action. Am I clear? Do you need a PowerPoint presentation on this? How can I make you understand?"

Rafael reached for a soggy fry. Cammie was having way too much fun with this. "You think this is a bad idea?"

"No," she said hastily. "I think it's a wonderful idea. We'll go and get all the stuff. You find someplace to stash it until you and Eve have that conversation. Sound good?"

Rafael studied his sister. She flashed him a devious little grin. "You're Tobias's kid, too," he said.

"I never said I wasn't." She stuffed her food in the to-go bag. "Come on! Let's get going!"

The sales assistant was handing out pink and blue sugar cookie samples from the bakery across the street. "For your next gender reveal party," she said.

Cammie declined. "I'm good."

"Yes, thanks," Rafael said. "I'll have hers, too."

"You've got a sweet tooth," Cammie observed. "I didn't know that."

Rafael took a bite of the blue cookie and grinned. "Now you know."

They wandered down the diaper aisle. "I'm so glad you're doing this. You have my full support."

"Thanks. That means a lot." Rafael paused to look around. "Think I might need some of these?"

"You can never have too many diapers, as I always say. Grab two sizes. That way you'll always be prepared."

Rafael did as instructed and loaded the cart.

"We'll need wipes. Lots of wipes."

He grabbed two packs of those.

"And maybe a Diaper Genie for cleanup."

"Seriously?"

"Trust me."

"You're a sweetheart, helping me like this. I'm not sure I deserve you."

"You probably don't." Cammie was rummaging through a bin filled with mini toy giraffes. "He likes to chew on these."

Rafael took the bin from her. "I'm trying to say thank you...for everything."

She offered him sunshine in a smile. "You're welcome...for everything."

He pulled his sister into a tight hug. "That was a lot of emotional heavy lifting."

"No kidding." She stretched up, kissed his cheek and snatched the blue cookie from him. "I'll take that, thanks."

Twenty-Four

Can a cookie heal a cracked heart? Eve wondered, staring into the display case filled with baked goodies. Maybe a cupcake? She was instantly drawn to the tres leches cupcakes topped with a strawberry nestled in a bed of creamy white icing. Why tres leches when her go-to cupcake was chocolate? She refused to answer that question and bought a whole pack of cupcakes instead of just one.

It was Wednesday. Eve had successfully avoided Rafael at work for two days straight. Or was he avoiding her? Either way, they were getting damn good at it. They kept open lines of communication via email but found ways to avoid face-to-face meetings or even run-ins by the elevators. Locking herself in her office was key. To avoid him at the residence, she locked herself in her suite. It was depressing as hell. The sooner she moved out, the better. Lately, her frequent calls to the real estate agent had gone unanswered. She was probably catering to more realistic clients.

Today Eve was going a little stir crazy, craving fresh air and sunshine. She slipped out during lunch and spent the hour window-shopping. When she came across the bakery, the buttery, sugary scents lured her in. She walked out with the pack of cupcakes. However, standing at the corner waiting for the light to change, a sense of hopelessness drilled through her.

A tres leches cupcake was not going to take the place of Rafael's sweetly addictive kiss. It just wasn't. Nothing would. She loved him. The quiet and simple realization wrapped itself around her, lifted her when she stepped out distractedly into the crosswalk just when a car shrieked to a stop inches away. The light hadn't yet turned red.

Rafael was at the wheel of a convertible with a large blue teddy bear in the passenger seat. She tried to blink the image away. This had to be a love-induced mirage.

"Lady!" he called out to her. "What are you doing?"

She took a step toward the vision. "You're real?"

"Get in this car!"

There wasn't any room. The teddy bear occupied the front seat and the back seat was crammed with boxes. A mini crib, a bouncy chair, diapers and more diapers. "Did you just rob a baby store? What is all this?"

The only possible explanation was that he was on his way to a baby shower. She stood back, waiting for him to confirm that the loot was for an acquaintance or an employee.

"These are for Micah."

Eve stopped breathing, certain her heart wasn't going to take it. "What do you mean? He doesn't need all this."

Rafael removed his sunglasses. Eve's heart took another stumble. She had never seen him looking so subdued. She wanted to climb over the large bear to get to him.

"I thought," he said haltingly. "If maybe you and Micah wanted to spend the night or a weekend, we'd be ready."

"Awww!"

What else was there to say? Her heart was melting. Had he gone off and made plans without first consulting her yet again? Yes, but they were the sweetest, most lovely plans, and she wanted to be a part of them. She saw it clearly in her mind's eye, and in her rose the desire to make the dream a reality.

"I want to make this work," he said. "I'll admit, I don't have any magic solutions, but I want to try. What do you think?"

"Well…I think you might have gone overboard. Did you keep the receipts? Some of these things can be returned."

"It's Cammie's fault. She piled stuff in the cart," he said. "Besides, you can never have too much. Babies need stuff, Eve. That's the first rule of baby."

"What about this huge teddy bear?" Eve cried. The thing had a head the size of a watermelon.

Rafael shrugged. "Drake said Micah loved teddy bears."

"A tiny one," she said. "Did you buy this extra-large one to out-teddy Drake's teddy?"

His grin turned devilish. "Exactly."

Eve rolled her eyes. "Men!"

Blaring horns interrupted their exchange. The light had turned red then green again. "Eve, get in this car."

"Get that bear out of the way."

Rafael grabbed the blue teddy and flipped him onto the back seat. She hopped in and they took off, wheels spinning. At the next light, he reached for her hand.

"What do you have there?" he asked, pointing to the bag.

"Sweets."

"Any caramel?"

"Nope," she said. "Tres leches cupcakes."

"Ah, sweet love," he said. "You missed me."

Eve tossed her head back and laughed. She'd missed him and the endless joy he brought to her life. He cupped her chin and drew her close. "I missed that laugh."

Her laughter died, quickly replaced by stillness. She had to say the words that were in her heart. She could not keep them locked away. "I love you, Rafael Arias Wentworth…whatever your name is."

His thumb swiped at a tear that had slipped out of the corner of her eye. He planted a kiss between her furrowed brows then gently, sweetly brushed his lips to hers. "I love you, too, darling," he whispered. "All your burdens are my burdens. All your problems are mine to solve. Everything you love, I love. From here on out, that is how it is, *mi amor*. Nothing can change that. Let me make you a home. It might not be conventional, but it would be for us."

A sailboat would feel like home if they were together. The room at an inn, her dreary efficiency, the residence at the guest ranch and the penthouse overlooking the Atlantic, any place they'd been together had felt like home. So long as Micah was welcome, she had no objections.

"Please say yes, my sweet."

Eve rushed to kiss him. "Like I can say no to you."

The honking resumed, more furious this time. Rafael growled like the wolf in black sheep's clothing that he was and put the car in motion.

"I think we deserve the afternoon off," he said. "Do you agree?"

"Absolutely!" Eve said. She kicked off her shoes. "Where to now?"

"The sunset."

"Where's that?" She'd never heard of the place. Was it a diner or a bar?

"We're in love," he said with that sparkle in his eyes. "We're driving into the sunset."

Epilogue

"I've called this meeting of the G-6 to inform you of some recent developments." Rafael sat at the corner of his desk and folded his arms across his chest, Eve at his side. Together, they faced Dan and Audrey, seated in the swivel chairs, and Bill and Lucas, standing behind them. "It's important to us that we keep everything aboveboard. We don't want to create any confusion."

"We also want to get ahead of any rumors," Eve added. "And we want everyone to feel comfortable."

"Any questions so far?" Rafael asked.

All four shook their heads. Dan glanced around the room, looking worried. Audrey gripped the armrest of her chair. Bill had gone pale. Lucas was snapping his gum. Rafael hurried to deliver the news before they imagined the worst. "Okay, here goes. I called you here to let you in on something. Eve and I are… We're in a relationship."

"We hope it doesn't make things weird," Eve said. "We will be as discreet as possible at work."

Rafael could feel her nervousness rush through him in waves. He draped an arm over her shoulders and tugged her close. She did not resist. So much for discretion!

This meeting had been her idea. She no longer wanted to sneak around, covering their tracks, and he didn't want things to get awkward at the office.

"Is that it?" Dan said.

"No, that's not it," Eve said. "We're moving in together. I'm moving into his suite. We will be living together, and my nephew will be staying with us part of the time. So…there's that."

"Wow!" Audrey let out a nervous laugh. "That's big news!"

"You'd think you guys were dropping a bombshell or something," Dan said flatly.

"I thought they were closing shop," Bill said, looking relieved. "Got me going there for a minute."

"You're in a relationship," Lucas said. "No shit?"

"Language!" Rafael scolded him.

"Yeah!" Dan said. "Show some respect."

Audrey was incensed. "Everybody *act* surprised!"

"Respectfully," Dan said, "we'll file this information in the 'no shit' folder."

Everyone broke out in hysterical laughter—everyone except Rafael and Eve. "You all are the worst," Rafael said.

"It was in the newspaper!" Audrey cried. "What do you expect?"

Eve covered her face with her hands. Rafael got up and cleared the room. "Everybody get back to work."

"Come on, everyone," Bill said. "You heard the boss."

"Congrats, you two!" Audrey said on her way out. "I knew it since day one."

"I called it," Lucas said.

They shuffled out of the office, shutting the door behind them. Eve turned to him, shaking with laughter. "Well... That was interesting. They were on to us this whole time."

"Looks like we were the only ones who weren't on to us," Rafael said.

"Seems anticlimactic, though," she said pensively. "Our big announcement fizzling out like that..."

Rafael frowned. Anticlimactic wasn't a word he wanted associated with their relationship. "We should do something to mark the occasion," he proposed. "What do you think?"

She snapped her fingers. "I know! Let's have sex on your desk. I've always wanted to."

There was his fearless Eve. Rafael slipped off his suit jacket. "Lock the door."

* * * * *

Don't miss the final installment in
Texas Cattleman's Club: Fathers and Sons
Available next month

The Rancher's Reckoning
by Joanne Rock

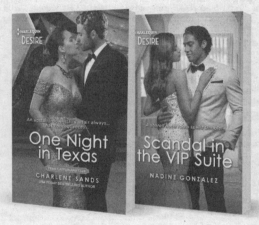

#2863 WHAT HAPPENS ON VACATION...
Westmoreland Legacy: The Outlaws • by Brenda Jackson
Alaskan senator Jessup Outlaw needs an escape...and he finds just the
right one on his Napa Valley vacation: actress Paige Novak. What starts
as a fling soon gets serious, but a familiar face from Paige's past may
ruin everything...

#2864 THE RANCHER'S RECKONING
Texas Cattleman's Club: Fathers and Sons • by Joanne Rock
Pursuing the story of a lifetime, reporter Sierra Morgan reunites a lost
baby with his father, rancher Colt Black. He's claiming his heir but
needs Sierra's help as a live-in nanny. Will this temporary arrangement
withstand the sparks and secrets between them?

#2865 WRONG BROTHER, RIGHT KISS
Dynasties: DNA Dilemma • by Joss Wood
As his brother's ex-wife, Tinsley Ryder-White is off-limits to Cody Gallant.
Until one unexpected night of passion after a New Year's kiss leaves
them reeling...and keeping their distance until forced to work together.
Can they ignore the attraction that threatens their careers and hearts?

#2866 THE ONE FROM THE WEDDING
Destination Wedding • by Katherine Garbera
Jewelry designer Danni Eldridge didn't expect to see Leo Bisset at
this destination-wedding weekend. The CEO once undermined her
work; now she'll take him down a peg. But one hot night changes
everything—until they realize they're competing for the same lucrative
business contract.

#2867 PLAYING BY THE MARRIAGE RULES
by Fiona Brand
To secure his inheritance, oil heir Damon Wyatt needs to marry by
midnight. But when his convenient bride never arrives, he's forced to
cut a marriage deal with wedding planner Jenna Beaumont, his ex.
Will this fake marriage resurrect real attraction?

#2868 OUT OF THE FRIEND ZONE
LA Women • by Sheri WhiteFeather
Reconnecting at a high school reunion, screenwriter Bailey Mitchell
and tech giant Wade Butler can't believe how far they've come and
how much they've missed one another. Soon they begin a passionate
romance, one that might be derailed by a long-held secret...

SPECIAL EXCERPT FROM

HARLEQUIN

DESIRE

After the loss of his brother, rancher Nick Hartmann is suddenly the guardian of his niece. Enter Rose Kelly— the new tutor. Sparks fly, but with his ranch at stake and the secrets she's keeping, there's a lot at risk for both...

Read on for a sneak peek at
Montana Legacy
by Katie Frey.

The ranch was more than a birthright—it was the thing that made him a Hartmann. His dad made him promise. Maybe Nick couldn't voice why that promise was important to him. Why he cared. His brothers shrugged the responsibility so easily, but he was shackled by it. His legacy couldn't be losing the thing that had made him. No. He couldn't fail at this. Not even to be with her, the mermaid incarnate.

She smiled her odd half smile and splashed some water at him again. "I don't think you even know all you want, cowboy." She bit her lip, drawing his attention instantly to the one thing he'd wanted since meeting her at the airport. He followed her in a second lap of the pool, catching up to her in the deep end.

"So your brother married your prom date?" She widened her eyes as she issued her question.

"It was a long time ago." He cleared his throat. Maybe Ben was right and he needed to open up a bit.

"Yes, you're practically ancient, aren't you?" She swatted a bit of water in his direction, which he managed to sidestep.

"Careful, Oxford." He smiled, unable to help himself. It felt good to smile, even more so when faced with the crushing sadness he'd been shouldering for the past three weeks.

"Can you not call me that?" She paused. "My sister went to Oxford. And I don't want to think about her right now."

Her bottom lip jutted forward and quivered. It provoked a response he was unprepared for, and he sealed her concern with a kiss so thorough it rocked him.

Everything he wanted to say he said with the kiss. *I'm sorry. I want you. I'm hurting. Let's forget this.* Her body, hot against his, was a welcome heat to balance the chill of the pool. It was soft and deliciously curved. The perfect answer to his desperate question.

His tongue parried hers and she opened to him with an earnestness that rocked him. A soft mew of submission and he lifted her legs around his, arousal pressed plainly against her. She wrapped her legs around him, the thin skin of the bathing suit a poor barrier, and bit gently at his lip.

"I'm sorry," he started.

"Let's not be sorry, not now." Gone was the sorrow. Instead, she looked at him with a burning fire that he matched with his own.

Don't miss what happens next in
Montana Legacy
by Katie Frey.

Available April 2022 wherever
Harlequin Desire books and ebooks are sold.

Harlequin.com

HDEXP0222

Love Harlequin romance?

DISCOVER.

Be the first to find out about promotions,
news and exclusive content!

Facebook.com/HarlequinBooks

Twitter.com/HarlequinBooks

Instagram.com/HarlequinBooks

Pinterest.com/HarlequinBooks

YouTube.com/HarlequinBooks

ReaderService.com

EXPLORE.

Sign up for the Harlequin e-newsletter and
download a free book from any series at
TryHarlequin.com

CONNECT.

Join our Harlequin community to
share your thoughts and connect
with other romance readers!
Facebook.com/groups/HarlequinConnection